HARD TIMES

NEUTRINOMAN AND LIGHTNINGIRL: A LOVE STORY,
EPISODE 5

ROBERT J. MCCARTER

LITTLE HUMMINGBIRD PUBLISHING

Hard Times

Neutrinoman and Lightningirl: A Love Story, Episode 5

Cover image: 123rf.com/profile_stokkete

Version 1.0, April 2020

ISBN: 978-1-941153-36-9

Find out more about this series at: Neutrinoman.com

Visit Robert's website at: RobertJMcCarter.com

Published by:

Little Hummingbird Publishing

P.O. Box 23518

Flagstaff, AZ 86002

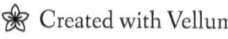 Created with Vellum

NEUTRINOMAN & LIGHTNINGIRL: A LOVE STORY

- Meteor Attack!
- Toxic Asset
- Protocol X
- Season 1 (Omnibus edition of Episodes 1 - 3)
- Off Book
- Hard Times
- Elemental Factors (coming June, 2020)
- Season 2 (Omnibus edition of Episodes 4-6, coming August , 2020)

Find out the latest at Neutrinoman.com

PROLOGUE: A SMALL CELL

I paced my cell counting the steps. One, two, three, four. Turned, paced the next wall. One, two, three, four. Turned, paced. Turned, paced.

I'm not Neutrinoman, I'm decidedly biological now, just Nik Nicholas, and have been since they brought me here. They made sure I didn't have enough power to transform.

I let my fingers slide over the smooth white walls where I can walk next to them. Past the narrow bunk, the metal toilet and sink, the tiny shower with a white plastic curtain, the shelf that has some toiletry items and the two books I have, and finally the workout wall. It's studded with a couple pull-up bars, a weight bench that folds up into the wall, and some free weights.

Twelve feet on a side, I knew these four walls much better than I should. I knew this cell so well that I hated every square inch of it. I took a deep breath, smelling the stale air and my own despair.

I stopped at the five-foot-wide section of my cell that was not two-foot-thick walls, but bars, a door. They were smooth and silvery, duller than steel, and much stronger, made out of some kind of exotic alloy. I could see thirty feet down the plain, unadorned hallway where it made an abrupt turn to the right. On the wall at the end of the hallway was a mirror and I saw myself reflected there. Short brown hair, fairly rumpled, medium height, medium build, dressed in bland grey coveralls.

I was just a man and I had been for over six months. I wasn't Neutrinoman flying out to save the Earth from an asteroid aimed at us by the Arcturian Alliance. I wasn't battling aliens to keep them from setting off the super volcano underneath Yellowstone National Park, and I wasn't trying and failing to stop Gaia in the form of a seven-hundred-foot-tall rock giant destroying the Hoover Dam.

I didn't have Lightningirl/Licia by my side. I wasn't alone, but I was so very lonely.

Behind that one-way mirror was a guard with one of the alien's energy weapons. It was always powered up. It was always pointed down the hall at me. Just in case I figured out how to transform into Neutrinoman. Just in case I tried to escape, they could easily stop me, the alien's weapon built just for me to sap my powers.

That turn in the hallway, that guard station, was only one of four getting to this cell.

I looked up at the ceiling twenty feet above me. It glowed evenly, light transferred here fiber-optically. There was not one joule of electricity anywhere I could reach to help power my transformation. Not one switch, one battery, nothing.

There was a TV hanging about fifteen feet down the hallway, but I have to ask a guard to turn it on or change the channel, so I didn't bother anymore.

I'm far underground in this prison built just for quantum metamorphs, q-morphs, like me. This cell built specifically for me. This had taken a lot of time to plan and build. The government must have started the process as soon as they found out about us and understood our powers and our weaknesses. The thought was a bitter taste in my mouth, like sucking on an aspirin.

I sighed, letting go of the cool bars of my cell door and kept on pacing. Kept on breathing. Kept on living.

What else could I do?

As prisons go, this was probably the best it could be. They fed me well, a kind man named Ronald brought me books, they had given me space and tools for exercise, but it was still a prison. It was still confinement. It was still punishment.

My fingers slid over my books as I paced past them, the noise loud in the silence, but comforting. Skin against paper. A rough splash of white noise. It sounded like freedom to me. And I don't mean freedom as in escaping into another world. I mean freedom as in getting out of these four walls. Real escape.

The books make me think of Licia, and the memory was so strong that I caught a whiff of her ozoney scent and saw a glimpse of her smile in my mind's eye. She would be happy that I've been reading so much. Before the military imprisoned me for "consorting with known terrorist, willful destruction of public property, blah, blah, blah," I had been more of a TV guy. But one of these books, it holds the key.

I'd been in here one hundred ninety days. I had a lot of time to read, to learn, to contemplate, to grow. I was almost there. I was close, I could taste it.

I was starving for freedom, for the wide-open sky, for Licia. I knew I'd be getting out one day, I knew I'd see her again. They'd either let me out or I would blast my way out. It was only a matter of time.

Escape was a simple, inevitable thing in my mind that day, but that's not the way it turned out. It wasn't a simple thing at all. I knew there would be a price to be paid, but I had no idea how hard it would be to bear.

1 / APPROACHING CHANGE

SUMMER 2025, CASITA DE SOLEDAD, CENTRAL ARIZONA

TIME PLAYS WITH ME AS I WRITE THESE MEMOIRS. AS I DANCE between past and present, reliving the past as I write and then coming back to the present, twenty years later after the war is long over and all the madness we all went though.

When I'm in the present, the past still lingers and Licia has been tolerant of the process, letting me ruminate and relive it all.

When I started these stories, I thought it would all be about the past with just a splash of the present, of Licia and I now to put things in context, to make us more real.

But one summer night in the hills near Casita de Soledad, our exiled home, it all changed.

We like to walk after dinner up a hill near our adobe home that we built with our own hands up onto a hill that gives a fine view of the rolling high desert so we can watch the sunset.

Our life was like that. Long walks. Time to talk. Plenty of time to sleep. We kept busy, continuing building here and my writing, but there was a gentle leisure to our days.

We were standing there holding hands watching the sun kiss the top of some craggy hills as it made its nightly journey.

"Someone's coming," I said. The third element of me acquiring my powers, after the cosmic rays that bathed the planet and the lethal dose of radiation I received, was the bite of a rat. It left me with very good hearing and an insatiable desire for cheese.

"Who is it?" Licia asked, her face close to mine, her breath smelling of curry, the low sun kissing her beautiful features.

I shook my head. "No idea. It's not time for a delivery, is it?"

"No," she said, shaking her head, her silky black hair sliding across her shoulders.

She hooked her arm in mine and leaned her head on my shoulder. She hadn't transformed into Lightningirl for a while, so I could smell soap and shampoo, not her usual ozone-laced scent.

It wasn't long until we saw two black SUVs slowly bouncing over the barely-there road that leads to our exile home. The view up here is vast, the dry land rolling away and diving into canyons, the dry dirt decorated with scrub brush, dried grass, and prickly pear cactus.

"It's got to be Homeland Security," I said. They are our current masters.

"But it can't be urgent," Licia said, "or they would have flown out."

"I doubt that it's anything good," I said. "It never is with them."

Several decades had passed since my imprisonment and countless challenges, but those days locked up had left me with a distrust of governmental authority. Those SUVs, as benign as their mission probably was, made me tense up. Made me remember that small cell and all that happened there.

I felt Licia nod, her silky hair rubbing against my arm.

We could leave. Licia could draw power from the high-tension power lines close by, transform into Lightningirl and then shoot lightning into me until I could transform into Neutrinoman. I could take her in my arms and fly her away from here.

But where would we go? And besides, I had gotten fed up with hiding. It was one of the reasons for the memoirs. It felt like it was time to be seen, time for our side of the story to be known. And it was time to meet whatever challenges those two SUVs were bringing and deal with it.

I laughed. It came out strained and too high pitched.

"What?" Licia asked.

"I'm worried about a couple of suits in SUVs. In the old days it would be Toxicwasteman, Gaia, or the Arcturian Alliance. Now I'm worried about agents."

She separated from me, her brown eyes searching mine in the rapidly dimming light. The sun had sunk below the horizon and was a fading glow on this cloudless night "Is that a good thing?" she asked.

I swallowed and studied her lovely face. It's round, her skin the color of creamed coffee and the most beautiful thing in the world to me. But she was serious, and I couldn't tell what kind of answer she wanted from me, so I stuck with the truth. "It's not a bad thing. I don't mind not having to save the world every other day. I just..." I shrugged weakly. "I don't trust them, Licia. "

She nodded, but I could tell she wasn't quite sure about my answer. "You're writing about your imprisonment now, aren't you?" she asked. I have never been able to hide anything from her.

I bit my lip and nodded. "I've been putting it off for a few weeks now, but I just started."

She pulled me into a fierce hug and held me tight while the SUVs slowly bounced closer. Our banishment here to Casita de Soledad, "The Lonely Little House," was implicit instead of a cell like they had locked me in.

"I'm here," she whispered.

"I know," I whispered back.

I held her and watched those SUVs as the sky darkened and the breeze brought the dry, dusty scent of the desert. The rumble of their engines was an intrusion to our quiet home, one that was more annoying than usual.

"We better go find out what they want," she said after a time.

"No more prison cells for me," I said, my voice surprisingly steady. "Never again."

She let go of me and took my hand. "No cells. Not with me here," she said quietly and led me towards what was sure to be change.

2 / DON'T FIGHT THIS

AFTER THE DISASTER AT HOOVER DAM WITH GAIA AND before they threw me in that cell, Colonel Williams put me in handcuffs and hauled me away. He did give me some fatigues to put on first, so at least I wasn't naked anymore.

Terrorism. Destruction of public property. Consorting with a known terrorist. I wasn't arrested. I was to be "detained." Which meant they were going to toss me in a deep hole and throw away the key.

Things had gone badly, very badly. Chaosboy and Toxicwasteman had warned us about Gaia and her plan to destroy the Hoover Dam. My new partner Quinn, Licia, and I had gotten there in time, but we hadn't been able to talk her out of it. She had transformed into a seven-hundred-foot-tall rock giant. We had fought. Gaia had been defeated, but the dam broke.

Toxicwasteman and I stopped the downstream flooding by blowing up enough rock to create a makeshift dam, but it wasn't enough for the military. The orders had come down, and Colonel

Williams had followed them. He put me in handcuffs and led me away.

The deal was that Quinn and Licia would stay free as long as Quinn used his q-morph powers to appear to be me and Licia played along.

That image of Licia is etched into my brain. She was dressed in oversized fatigues and standing on the reddish rock in front of the bland green military tent. As the UH-1 helicopter lifted off, I could see the Hoover Dam behind her, water still spilling out the huge gash, a temporary Niagara Falls in the dry desert. Quinn was standing a few paces behind her, and despite his bulk compared to her petiteness, I could only see her. The wind of the rotors tossing her silky black hair about, her hand was to her forehead shielding her eyes from the rising sun. A look of grim determination and fear alternately playing on her face.

I had fought for her, for us, and we had finally been together, finally a couple. And now this.

"Can you hear me? We don't have much time," Williams said in his gravelly baritone as we flew away. The noise in the helicopter was overwhelming. The thump of the rotors, the howling of the wind. Neither of us had headsets on and I could only hear him because of the enhanced hearing. Williams knew all about my abilities.

I looked at him, but he wasn't looking at me, instead staring in the other direction. His face turned away from the two soldiers in the back of the helicopter with us. I gave a slight nod and kept staring at Licia. I could barely see her, but I wasn't about to look away, not until her tiny form disappeared completely.

"Don't fight this, Nik," he said, his hand brushing at his short salt-and-pepper hair. "There are some, plenty actually, that are scared of you. No, terrified. That are hoping you do fight this. They are looking for any excuse."

I gave another nod, just so he was sure I was listening.

"You are powerful," he continued, "and if they can't control you, they would rather destroy you, the alien threat be damned."

I bit my lip. I couldn't see Licia anymore, but I kept staring at the rough reddish-brown land where she had been.

"I won't be with you much longer," Williams continued. "Remember what I've said when it gets bad. And it will get bad. I will do everything I can for you from the outside."

I wanted so badly to turn, to look him in the eyes, to express some sliver of gratitude. But I didn't. I sat there staring at the desert, terrified of what was coming next.

FROM HOOVER DAM, THE HELICOPTER FLEW US OVER LAKE Mead. I didn't enjoy the stark, eroded landscape or marvel at the beauty of that much water in the middle of the dry desert. The handcuffs were tight and felt heavier than they should. Williams wasn't talking, his jaw set, his eyes never meeting mine. He didn't like this, but he was a soldier, he followed orders.

But I wasn't a soldier. I thought of jumping out of the Huey. Transforming into Neutrinoman, melting those damn handcuffs off, flying back to Licia. Maybe finding Toxicwasteman and letting him hide us.

It was a distasteful vision, but not as distasteful as "detainment." It was the colonel's warning that stopped me.

A few miles north of the lake in a desolate stretch of flat desert, the helicopter touched down. There was another UH-1 waiting for me there full of soldiers not dressed in uniforms, but dressed in black. Black sunglasses, black cotton pants, black long-sleeved shirts, black ballistic vests with fat pockets, thick belts with a gun and pouches hanging on them, all of them looking alike but for the different shades of their hair and slightly different heights.

Williams guided me out of the helicopter, one strong hand around my right bicep.

Two men got out of the other helicopter. They were beefy and square jawed, looking kind of like marines to me (or at least how I imagined marines looked if you dressed them all in black).

"You boys treat him well," Williams said to the soldiers in black, "or you'll be answering to me on down the line."

With that he left me standing there and got back into the UH-1. I turned and gave him an awkward salute—handcuffs, you know—as the helicopter lifted off. He saluted me back. I watched until the helicopter was out of sight.

When I turned back all four of the soldiers were out of the helicopter. Two of them held the alien energy weapons, the ones that drain my power. Without a word they began firing.

The bolts didn't exactly hurt, I wasn't in my neutrino form, but I did feel my reserves quickly fade. I couldn't have transformed into Neutrinoman if I had tried.

The big one, the one who seemed to be the leader, came forward and threw a black bag over my head and I was roughly loaded into the helicopter and we took off. No one said a word.

The bag stunk of oil, and in that darkness with only the roar of the helicopter to keep my company, I felt despair. This "detainment" was looking to be worse than I imagined.

———

THE HELICOPTER RIDE WASN'T LONG. I WAS THEN transferred to the back end of a C-5 transport and the bag removed from my head. We had to be at Nellis Air Force Base, which sits on the northeast corner of Las Vegas.

My four square-jawed, beefy companions were still there. They didn't talk to me, they just watched me, one of them always had an alien energy weapon trained on me, and another always had a pistol pointed at me.

We took off. There were no windows and I felt the plane shift course multiple times. This, I suspected, they were doing for me. Making sure I didn't know where we were going. And I didn't.

We were in the air for five hours, and believe me, this was a long five hours. I felt like a teenager sitting outside the principal's office, waiting for my punishment. I kept going over what had happened with Chaosboy and Gaia and Toxicwasteman. Could I have prevented the destruction of the dam? Should I have attacked Gaia right away, as Tom had suggested in the video he had left me at the Golden Nugget? What would have happened if Quinn, in his Hammer form, hadn't charged Gaia? It had seemed like we were getting through to her.

But the more I thought about it, the more I began to realize it wasn't the Hoover Dam that had pissed them off. It was that Chaosboy had gotten away. That Toxicwasteman had gotten away. That I really didn't even try to bring Toxicwasteman in. That I wasn't playing by their rules anymore.

I believed that Tom Tyree (aka Toxicwasteman) was a sociopath, I also believed that he was hell-bent on destroying the aliens and that we needed him if we were going to have any chance of winning this fight.

I didn't feel sorry for letting him go. And I knew that was not the right mental state when waiting for punishment. They would want me recalcitrant, sorry for what I had done, that I had strayed from the path.

But I wasn't sorry.

This was no high school principal I was waiting for, though. This was serious.

3 / AN OLD FRIEND

It was dark and Licia and I were waiting outside our little adobe home when the two SUVs pulled up. Agent Peters got out of the backseat of the lead SUV. He was dressed in his usual black suit with a dour frown on his face.

He was generally the lead agent when we had visits. Licia's managed to develop a good rapport with him, but we don't talk. I hate the look of his bald head and thin lips. I hate what he represents.

But this time, something was different. His shoulders were slumped as he walked around the SUV and opened the other passenger-side door. An old man dressed in jeans and a cowboy shirt got out.

"Thanks, son," the old man said to Peters who nodded and pointed to the rear SUV and then to our house.

The old man's voice was rough, like sandpaper on metal, but still strong and he stood erect. Two agents, a man and a woman, both young, leapt out of the rear SUV and started carrying things towards our house. An olive-green duffle sack and a few cardboard boxes.

I was still putting it together, steeped in worry about an agent visit. But not Licia. She squealed with delight and ran to the old man, embracing him.

Colonel Williams. It had been twenty years since I met him and, unlike Licia and I, time had extracted its usual price. He was now in his mid-seventies with snow-white hair and a deeply wrinkled and leathery face. But he still had his usual brush cut and his piercing green eyes, and aside from a mild widening around the middle he looked as fit as usual.

"Colonel," I said after I walked over, a wide smile cracking my face. You don't go through what all of us did and survive and not have feelings for each other. I couldn't have been happier to see him.

Licia had him by the hand and was talking rapidly. "Are you hungry? We've got some leftover curry I can heat up. No meat, of course, but it's good. You always liked my cooking. God, I'm glad to see you. What are you doing here?"

When she stopped to take a breath, Williams laughed. It was a happy thing and I felt the tension in my shoulders melt away. "I'm here," he said, "because Sunni kicked me out."

"What?" Licia said, her brow crinkling in worry. "Is there anything wrong?"

"No. No. We're fine. Retirement is... well... I'm not so good at it. I was starting to get on her nerves, so she told me to go find something to do for a few days."

"Well, you're welcome here," Licia said. She was still bubbly, a smile lighting up her face. "Any time. As long as you like." Clearly Licia needed some company. We were just so isolated out here.

"Yes, Colonel," I added. "As long as you like. Or should I say General." I was truly glad to see him. Because I too needed the company, I genuinely liked and respected the man, and I could ask him some questions to help my storytelling along.

"For Christ's sake, Nik," he said, clapping me on the shoulder. "Call me Walter, will you. I'm neither a colonel nor a general now, and we've been through far too much for such formality."

Our eyes met when he said it. We were still standing under the starlight, agents moving about us, hauling what Williams had brought into our house. He sounded happy, he looked happy, but his eyes were telling a different story. There was something else going on here. Something else behind his visit.

I shook it off, chalking the paranoia up to old habits from the old days, from revisiting my time in that twelve-by-twelve cell.

"It's good to see you, Walter," I said, embracing him.

His still-strong arms held me tightly and longer than I expected. There was a slight tremor, maybe a shiver, as he held me. Maybe he was just old, but it convinced me there was something else. Something worthy of the worry.

4 / PRISON

I TOLD MY INTERROGATOR THE TRUTH—WELL, ALMOST ALL OF the truth. I told him that Quinn and I had headed to Vegas specifically to capture Chaosboy. That I feared what he could do and how casually he did it. I told him that he had warned us about Gaia, that Tom Tyree / Toxicwasteman had left us a briefing in the suite of the Golden Nugget. That I had enlisted Licia to help us and kept the military out of it.

We were underground, how far I couldn't say, but it was a long ways. The elevator ride had taken a few minutes. I was alone in the room, a plain square box with white walls and one metal chair.

This was before I saw my cell and my first interrogation. There was a camera pointed at me and the voice of my interrogator came out of some speakers mounted on the wall. He wasn't in the room with me. I couldn't see his face, which was starting to bug me.

"You don't trust us?" he asked, his voice smooth and calm. He sounded like he should be narrating audio books or something.

"I trust some of you," I answered.

"What does that mean?" he asked.

"It means I've worked with people in the government I would trust with my life," I said, taking a breath of the stale air. "But the organization as a whole? Not really, no."

"Then why didn't you leave the program like Miss Lopez?" he asked.

"Is that an option now?" I said, flashing a sarcastic grin at the camera.

"No."

I was dressed in grey coveralls and had thick handcuffs made of that dark grey metal on both my wrists and my ankles. My square-jawed friends had stripped me down, executed a rather intimate search, and had put me in the jumpsuit and matching accessories. I didn't resist. It wouldn't have done any good.

"Was it an option then?" I asked.

The voice was silent. I imagined him, my interrogator, switching off the microphone and conferring with the other men in a little room next to this one. My interrogator, as I saw him in my mind's eye, was short and bald, with pale brown eyes and a weak chin. I had no idea what he looked like, it just helped me to imagine him that way.

"Let's go back to when Chaosboy got away," he finally said, ignoring my question. "He just jumped off the roof?"

I knew he knew the answer. We had been closely observed in Las Vegas. "I'm sorry I didn't try to leave the program," I said, ignoring his question as he had ignored mine. "Licia is smarter than me. Much smarter. But I guess the reason I stayed is I believe in what we are fighting for."

"And what is that?" the voice asked.

The smile I gave the camera took effort. It was like swallowing a bitter pill without any water. "Freedom. Freedom from the aliens. Freedom to determine our own fate."

Silence again. They must be conferring. "Do you still believe in that? The fight for freedom?"

I smiled, this time easier. "I will always believe in that."

———

IT SEEMED TO BE A KIND OF GENTLEMAN'S PRISON. No violence. No torture. And almost no human contact except for Ronald, the man who brought me books.

The interrogations happened daily for the first two weeks. Each morning three of those square-jawed, beefy boys would escort me to the little room. They all had mirror shades on and they never said a word.

One would point an alien energy weapon at me with its metal tube and bulky backpack. They still had a jerry-rigged look to them. Another one would have a handgun pointed at me, and the third would have a pair of handcuffs on a long pole. They weren't fooling around. After the cuffs were on, they'd escort me a ways down that winding hallway to the little room.

There I would sit and talk to that smooth, disembodied voice. He asked me the same questions over and over. It was boring, and I think that was the point. That big-bellied, little bald guy—as I imagined him—was trying to break me through sheer boredom. Like if he just asked the question enough times, I might answer it differently.

After about a week I just stopped answering. We had been over it. I told them almost everything. I left out the conversation that Toxicwasteman and I had had after stopping the flood waters from the broken Hoover Dam, and I left out the location of the real LoVE base I had been at.

The rest of it, including my belief that we needed Tom and his crew, I was totally upfront about. But that smooth voice kept digging, so I stopped talking.

After a week of me not talking, things changed. Right after one of the beefy boys delivered my dinner, I met Ronald, an older, elegant-looking black man.

He wasn't dressed that elegantly in tan slacks and a black T-shirt, but it was more the way he moved. There was a grace to his walk, an elegance in his long fingers and thin limbs. He looked to be around seventy with his hairline having receded back to a strip of short white hair. I was surprised to see him.

"Who are you?" I asked, slumped on my bunk. I was so bored, I had nothing to do but workout, sleep, and refuse to talk to the smooth-voiced man. No books, and I was sick of TV and the endless commercials. In truth, I had slipped way past boredom into a deep depression.

"My name is Ronald," he said, extending his hand through the bars.

I was shocked. No one had talked to me since I got to this place, not face to face. "Um... yeah..." I got up and shook his hand. His grip was firm and his hands were rough, as if he did a lot of manual labor. "I'm Nik."

"Is there anything you need?" he asked.

It took me a moment. After two weeks of silence—except for the damn interrogations—I found it hard to speak. "Umm... I don't know... a book would be nice."

Ronald smiled and nodded and walked slowly down the hall. I found myself smiling as I ate my food, remembering how Ronald's hand had felt, his white-toothed smile, his deep, reassuring voice.

The next day in interrogation instead of being silent, I asked, "Who's Ronald?"

The room was intentionally bland. White walls. Metal chair. The only thing of interest to look at was the white camera facing in in one of the corners. The air was stale and warm. There was nothing of interest in this room but the conversation.

There was silence on the other end, like he was conferring with someone. "Who do you think he is?" the smooth-voiced man asked.

Another surprise. I had tried to steer the conversation in a different direction many times, but it had never worked. "I... I think he's a spy." I was kind of surprised to hear the words tumble out. I hadn't been consciously thinking it, but it made sense. "He's ex-CIA or something. You are hoping I open up to him."

Another bit of silence. "Let's go back to when Tom Tyree tried to recruit you. What exactly did he say to you while you were in their base at the Grand Canyon? Try to remember every word."

I had come to hate that voice. It was too calm, too smooth, too in control. "He said the military would eventually do something stupid and that I couldn't let it take me out of the game."

"But you are out of the game now," the voice said.

"Am I?" I asked.

Silence again. This conversation wasn't a fair one. They had a camera on me, they were, undoubtedly, studying my face, gleaning more information than I was giving them verbally. I couldn't see the person (or rather, I suspected, persons) on the other end.

"You look like you are out of the game to me," he said.

"Maybe the game has changed. Maybe I want to be here." And yes, I should have known better. I should have learned my lesson about picking a fight on someone else's turf from my interview with Diane Madison. But I was sick of this. I felt trapped and powerless. I wanted out. If all that was left to me was a verbal game, I was going to try something.

"Why would you want to be here?"

"The food," I said, "and the companionship. It's excellent." This verbal game wasn't me, and that was a problem. Tom, now he could do this kind of thing all day and love it, but me, I only had a bit of sarcasm as defense.

"Let's go back to when Tom Tyree tried to recruit you. What exactly did he say to you while you were in their base? Try to remember every word." He said it exactly the same way he had the time before. The same words, the same intonation. It was maddening.

I just shook my head and didn't say another word.

Their plan wasn't clear. What did they intend to do to me in this "gentle" prison? Just feed me and interrogate me and then expect me to go fight for the planet if the aliens returned?

I could see no way out and my only hope was that Ronald would talk to me again, would bring me a book, would help break the monotony before it broke me.

5 / BREAKING THE LAW

THE FIRE CRACKLED, THE STARS SPARKLED, AND WALTER Williams and I drank.

After we had gotten him settled in our guest room at Casita de Soledad and he had eaten—and thoroughly praised—some of Licia's curry, he had grabbed a mason jar out of one of the cardboard boxes and said, "Come on, Nik, get drunk with an old friend, will you?"

"What is that?" I asked.

"Whiskey. Homemade. Sunni, she said to me after I retired, 'You better get a hobby, Walt, or we'll be getting a divorce.'" He paused, a wide grin on his angular face. "Not that she entirely approves of *this* hobby."

He invited Licia too, but she declined, saying she had to clean up. I think we all knew she was going to call Sunni and make sure things were okay between them.

I took Williams out to our flagstone patio. It juts out from the front of our house, has a built-in firepit, and a hell of a view of our high-desert home during the day and a stunning view of the stars at night.

There are no cities near Casita de Soledad. Most nights, and this was one, you can see the milky way above, a dense swath of stars strewn against the dark velvet void.

I lit the fire and Williams poured us drinks.

"To the fallen," he said, raising his glass to the stars. "May the sonofabitch aliens never come back, and may you be here if they do to kick their grey asses once again."

"To the fallen," I echoed, our glasses clinking as I shot the tea-colored liquid down. It burned my throat and I coughed like some kid taking his first shot of hard liquor.

Williams slapped me on the back and chuckled. "It's not the smoothest drink you'll ever have."

"You ain't kidding," I said when I could talk again.

"I have not mastered the art," he said while he refilled our little shot glasses. "But it's a hell of a lot better than my first attempt, and it gets the job done."

The warmth was spreading into my stomach and I felt my shoulders further relaxing. I took measured sips while Williams knocked the whiskey back.

He was sitting hunched over a bit, his right hand against his chest moving in an odd pattern. It took me a moment to realize that he was signing. American Sign Language had been part of our training with the military. It provided useful numerous times, like when we were out of the atmosphere and couldn't speak, or around enemies and needed to talk privately.

He was only using a single hand and was spelling out a single word. *Danger*.

When my eyes widened in recognition, my mouth opening to speak, he said, "Think about it, son." He then took a breath before adding, "I haven't been doing this long, so I'm not going to be that good at it. On Sunni's insistence, I did pull some strings and get a license to do this, so at least I'm not..." He trailed off, for just a second, like he had drunk a bit too much, but I knew he hadn't. He finally finished, a serious look on his grizzled face "...breaking the law.

He was asking me to think about why he was signing to me and was he telling me he was breaking the law? I closed my mouth, feeling the tension crawl back into my shoulders, and took another sip of the rot-gut whiskey.

He was signing again, this time with two hands, his back to the desert, hunched over a bit. *You must get drunk. It's important.*

I nodded and shot back the rest of the whiskey. Colonel Williams was here passing secret messages, breaking the law, why the hell not get drunk?

6 / EATING EGGS AND DRINKING COFFEE

I THINK I WOULD HAVE LOST IT DOWN THERE WITHOUT Ronald. Every time I saw him ambling down the long hallway, I smiled. He had this presence to him that reminded me of the seventy-ish Morgan Freeman. Not that he looked like Freeman; Ronald was bald with only a strip of white hair remaining, and rather homely looking. It was more the vibe he put off. Like he was a man that you could trust.

"Special delivery," he said that next morning after I had met him. My breakfast had just arrived, runny eggs, underdone toast, and cold coffee. The lock rattled on the pass-through I got my meals from. It was a beat-up hardback book. *Killing Floor* by Lee Child.

"It's the first Jack Reacher novel," Ronald offered. "I think you'll like it. Reacher is a man of action, kind of like you."

"Thanks, Ronald. But... How... Why are they letting me have books now?"

He just smiled and shrugged his shoulders. "Enjoy," he said as he ambled back down the hallway.

I sat there on my bunk holding the scarred book while my food got cold. The spine was broken, the cover ragged, and the pages a bit yellow. The book had been well used. I cracked it open, flipped to the first page and started reading:

I was arrested in Eno's diner. At twelve o'clock. I was eating eggs and drinking coffee.

I looked over to my eggs and coffee and felt a chill go down my spine. The coincidence seemed bizarre. Did Ronald know I had just received the food the book opened up with?

When I was young, I had read a lot. Mostly fantasy, things like *The Lord of the Rings* and it's progeny. But when I hit college, that had stopped in favor of studying. And after college and Ashley when I entered my coasting phase, I never took it back up.

With its short sentences and quick pace, the book was clearly a thriller of some sort. I started reading, my breakfast forgotten. It was such a relief to escape that cell—even if only in my mind—for a while.

A few hours later, at the top of chapter 13, was a note scrawled in bright red ink:

"Hold on. We're making a plan. Will come if they don't let you out. Look to my boy, Ron."

It was signed with two looping Ts. Tom Tyree. It had to be him.

I slammed the book shut and put it down on my bunk. My eyes darted around the cell. Where exactly were the cameras? Was there any chance that they had seen that? Should I tear the page out and flush it? No, no. That would just bring more attention to it.

So Ronald wasn't CIA or even working for the government. Ronald was sent here by Tom.

I knew the emotions I was feeling were all over my face so I got on my rowing machine and started working out. The rowing machine, like everything in this cell had no electricity, no power. It had a handle that you pulled back that moved a fan. Nothing special, but at least I could get an aerobic workout.

My mind was reeling. What would it mean if LoVE came and

got me? How many would die for my freedom? Could I live with that?

The walls of the cell were a boring white. No color. No pictures. Nothing. Before Ronald all I had to keep me sane was exercising, and it was clear that wasn't going to be enough. But if Ronald was Tom's "boy," how did he get in here? How were they letting him talk to me and bring me a book?

After the workout I pulled the little plastic curtain around the tiny shower area and let the hot water run over me for a long time. Tom Tyree and his boy Ron were my lifeline down here. Tom Tyree was saving me... again.

Once I was clean and dressed, I went back to the book. I had decided to do nothing about the note written in chapter 13. I kept my face calm and opened the book back up and when I got to chapter 13, I gasped.

That red ink was gone. I flipped back, looking through each chapter page until I got to the beginning, but didn't find it. I then flipped forward, but it wasn't there either.

I did my best to calm myself. I hadn't imagined the note, had I?

———

AFTER KILLING FLOOR, RONALD BROUGHT ME DIE TRYING AND then *Tripwire*. All Jack Reacher novels. I would gobble them up in a day or two, going back and rereading my favorite parts.

I did my best to keep track of days, but without a pen or even something sharp to scrape on the walls, I lost track of time, but I had a feeling that spring had slipped into summer.

My daily interrogation sessions with the smooth-voiced man continued, but I had strength again. I started asking more questions and refused to answer his. We had strange little conversations.

"When are you letting me go?" I asked one day.

"When you answer all my questions," he replied.

"But I have."

"No you haven't," he said.

"Okay, what question haven't I answered?" I asked.

"This woman that worked for Tom Tyree, this 'Byte.' What is her real name?"

"I can't answer that question because I don't know the answer," I said.

"No one ever used another name for her? A nickname?" he asked.

"No."

"And you don't know anything else about her? Where she's from, where she worked, how she got her powers?" he asked.

"No," I lied. That was one other area I had been less than truthful about. No one knew who Byte was—my gut told me it needed to stay that way. "I didn't interact with her all that much."

"But you robbed a train together," he said.

"That we did," I replied. "It was fun."

"And you never had a private conversation with her?" he asked.

"A few, but not about anything private," I said.

"I don't believe you," he said.

"I don't care," I said.

Those books were making me stronger. Jack Reacher was one tough son of a bitch. He wouldn't take this faceless man's crap, and neither would I. The books and the sliver of human contact with Ronald had changed things for me.

I suspected they had enough equipment trained on me to tell when I was lying and when I wasn't. But I didn't care about that either.

There was one thing that didn't make sense. Ronald and his books had given me this strength. Even if Ronald was working for Tom, why are they letting him talk to me? It didn't make sense.

"Who is Ronald?" I asked after a minute of silence.

He didn't reply right away, once again. "Who do you think he is?"

"I don't know," I said.

Another long silence. "What have you been reading?" the voice asked.

"Jack Reacher novels. Ronald brought them to me." At first, I felt guilty telling him, like I'm ratting Ronald out or something. But they have to know what he's doing. They're watching, always watching. "Is he some sort of librarian?" I asked.

"Is that what you think he is?" the voice asked.

I shrugged my shoulders. "Maybe now, but I don't think he was always one."

"What do you think he was before he was a librarian?" he asked.

"A spy... no, maybe a diplomat," I said. "He's a very trustworthy kind of a guy. But it doesn't really matter, I've told you everything, so sending him in to try to get more out of me is just a waste of time."

This game was dangerous and I needed that. Part of me believed that the note written on chapter 13 of *Killing Floor* was real, that somehow Tom had turned someone down here. And another part of me thought that I had just imagined it, that maybe I wasn't doing as well as I thought, that I was slowly losing myself.

Silence, I again imagined my pudgy and bald interrogator conferring with people. "Maybe we should stop his visits," he finally said.

My heart started thumping in my chest, like it was trying to escape the prison of my body. I didn't know if I could take it if Ronald didn't come by, didn't bring me books. I swallow hard. "Your choice," I said, trying to sound casual and failing utterly.

"We'll take it under advisement," the voice said.

SUMMER 2025, CASITA DE SOLEDAD, CENTRAL ARIZONA

BY THE TIME LICIA JOINED US OUTSIDE, THE FIRE WAS burning nicely and Williams and I were drunk. He hadn't signed much more to me, but kept me drinking just enough to be drunk, but not enough to get too stupid.

It was a beautiful night, the fire chasing away the chill and the stars resplendent and bright in our isolated location. Earlier the yips of coyotes had bounced across the rolling desert land.

"Licia!" I cried when she came out. She had a grey sweater pulled tight around her and looked serious. "Come have some of Walter's wonderful whiskey." I giggled at the rhyme. I had drunk enough that I was actually liking it now.

"I don't think so," she said to me and then looked to Williams. "Sunni says to take it easy on the whiskey."

"Well Sunni's not here, is she?" Williams said, his eyes narrowing and looking around at the shadows around us. He then looked very serious. "She's not here, is she?"

"She's worried about you," Licia said, her arms crossed. "You've been preoccupied, restless. And at this point, I'm worried about both of you."

"We're just having a little fun," I said, my words slurring more than I wanted them to. "We don't have enough fun around here."

Licia's eyes met mine briefly, her lips a thin line.

I made an exaggerated nod of my head, indicating that I wanted her to look at my hands. I was hunched over, just like Williams had been and I signed, *Something is going on. We are in danger.*

Licia's eyes widened, and her mouth opened to speak, but Williams lurched up and put his arm around her. "You won't refuse to have a drink with your old friend, will you? I made this whiskey with my own two hands and you can't refuse me."

Licia looked back to me, confused. If there was danger, why were we getting drunk? Williams was sitting back down and signed, *I must tell you both something important, you must drink first.*

Licia sighed and sat down, pulling one of our patio chairs up next to Williams. "Okay, one drink. But only one." And then she signed, *Why drink?*

So they don't hear the stress in your voices when I say what I need to say, Williams signed.

Licia took the proffered whiskey and shot it back. She gasped but didn't cough like I had.

Who? I signed. *There is no one out here.*

Williams gave me a grim smile as he refilled all three of our glasses. The air was thick with the smell of smoke and the tang of alcohol. "To the fallen," he said, raising his glass, repeating the toast he had done with me earlier. "For those that died so that we might live."

"Hear, hear!" Licia cried.

After we drank, Williams signed, *Homeland Security. They listen to every word you two say.*

"I think I'll take another," Licia said, the flickering yellow of the fire making her look fierce.

Licia quickly joined us in our drunkenness and then Williams told us what he had come here to tell us.

8 / HER FACE

SUMMER 2005, LOCATION UNKNOWN

FOUR WALLS. FOOD TO EAT. MEANS TO EXERCISE. FACELESS sessions with the voice.

I don't think I ever imagined a prison to be like this, and if I had, I wouldn't have understood the difficulties of it. I see one of those beefy square-jawed guards twice a day when they bring my meals, and three times a day when they escort me to my interrogation, but they never speak to me, and they have on dark sunglasses so there is never the possibility of eye contact.

They were depriving me of human contact, of real interaction. Isolating me. Giving me one, and only one, avenue of expression, my interrogations.

A week of that seemed easy. I worked out, caught up on sleep, enjoyed the verbal banter of the interrogations, ate my food.

At four weeks it was starting to get hard. I felt myself wanting to treat my faceless interrogator as my friend. To talk to him like a friend. To tell him things. But I resisted.

Eight weeks in and I woke up one morning and couldn't remember what Licia looked like. I had been having a dream where

I wandered through an empty Phoenix, cars parked on the freeway, houses vacant with the doors open and the TVs on, no one home, not even a cat or a dog. Just emptiness under a blazing hot summer sun.

I found myself, after walking for what seemed like days, at my parents' house. The place where I had grown up and the place my parents had had to abandon when Diane Madison revealed my identity. The front door was open and I walked in calling for my mother and my father. I could smell my mother's cheap perfume and the house was clean, everything put away, like someone was living there.

I rushed through, opening doors, checking in the garage and finding my Dad's 1972 Dodge Charger, but not my parents.

I went into my bedroom and flopped onto my little twin bed. This was my room when I was a kid and is still very much like it had once been. The shelf of Star Wars models I had built as a kid. A few trophies from my time running cross country in high school. A picture of me and Robby Holmes, my best friend in high school and college, with our cap and gown on at our high school graduation. And a picture of me and a dark-haired woman.

I'm puzzled by the picture. It's just a normal picture, but for some reason I can't see the woman's face. It's not like it's blurred out or anything, it's just that my mind doesn't register it.

I can see that she's got long black hair, she's wearing a red tank top with a yellow lightning bolt emblazoned on it. I'm sitting close to her, a big goofy smile on my face. You can see part of my forearm, it's a selfie. We're sitting on a picnic table and you can see a hill rising in the distance behind us with noticeable horizontal lines running across the hill.

That's a vineyard on that hill. I know that place. It's a winery in the Verde Valley that sits right on Oak Creek. I've been there... with...

It was a dream and my mind was sluggish, trying to grapple with the feelings of isolation. I know that woman, her name is...

Lisa? No, that's not it. Alice? No, it doesn't start with "A." I sit down on my bed holding the picture, still not able to see the face. She's beautiful, I know that. And petite. Powerful, she's somehow very powerful.

I feel tears running down my face. For this lost world I am trapped in, for this woman that I know I love but can't remember, for this ache in my heart.

When I woke up, my heart was pounding and real tears were running down my real cheeks. I rolled over on my bed, facing the smooth wall, pulling the thin blanket over my head. I didn't want them to see me cry.

And as my mind went over the strange dream, I knew that girl's name. It was Licia. It was Lightningirl. My love. My reason for holding on. My reason for going to this prison without a fight. My reason for getting up in the morning.

Licia Lopez. Beautiful black hair and thick eyebrows, coffee and cream-colored skin, deep brown eyes.

But I couldn't put those features together. I closed my eyes shut and I couldn't "see" her. I bolted upright, too freaked out to care about my watchers. I began pacing my cell trying to force my mind to see her. It'd been eight weeks—how could her image have faded so fast? What was wrong with me?

Silky black hair. A slightly turned-up nose. A round face.

But these were just words, the image wouldn't come to me. I knew I was losing it, that my isolation had worn me down. But knowing it didn't help me stop my tumble.

The next time the voice asked me what I hadn't told him, I was going to spill it. I was going to tell him everything I know about Byte. About the real location of the LoVE base where Tom Tyree left me a supply of uranium ore. About the conversation we had after Gaia breached the Hoover Dam.

All of it would come spilling out of me. I would trade it for a picture of Licia. She felt like she's slipping away and I couldn't stand that.

9 / PROJECT VULCAN

Under the stars, we three were drunk, Colonel Williams, Licia, and me. Our drinking slowed but we all stayed at that balance point. Definitely drunk, but some control remaining.

The fire popped and sparked, a cool breeze kicked up from the west, and the stars continued to dazzle.

Williams signed to us as we drank and talked about silly things. He told us about project "Vulcan." When we had moved out here in 2021, the land had been prepared for us. The rudimentary road built. The foundation for our casita laid. A well drilled. And one more thing.

They had buried a bomb below us. It was called Project Vulcan. It was a failsafe. If we became a threat or too much trouble, they would trigger the bomb and we would be gone.

This was why Williams had insisted we be drunk. We were chatting, having the conversation old war buddies might have, but below all of this was the serious talk of impending doom. The slurred speech of the intoxicated was—Williams was hoping—enough to mask the stress of what he was telling us.

I threw another log on the fire, crackling sparks rising briefly into the night, throwing too much light on our grim faces.

"I can see why Sunni frowns on this little hobby of yours," Licia said while signing, *Why would they do this?*

We all signed carefully, our bodies leaning towards the fire, our backs facing the desert, our hands in front of our abdomens. We knew they were watching.

"That she does," Williams said. "But she told me to find something to occupy my time. This does it two ways. While I make it and while I drink it." *Humans fear what they can't control, what is more powerful than they are. You two are both.*

"Well I think it's the best damn whiskey I've ever had," I said. *What do we do now?*

"That's the booze talking, son," Williams said. "It's terrible whiskey, but not as bad as my first batch." *I have a plan.*

What is it? Licia signed.

"Ahh hell," Williams said as he poured the last drop from the mason jar into his glass. "This one is empty." *Time to dig that root cellar. Time for Nick to remember some old skills.*

"I'll get us another one," I said, rising to my feet, my body swaying like I was a sailor on choppy seas. *Root cellar? Skills?*

"No," Williams said. "This old man is tired. It's a hell of a bumpy trip out here." *In the morning tell me about where you plan to dig your root cellar. I know you've been planning it. Dig where I tell you not to.*

With a groan he got up, putting his hand on Licia's shoulder to steady himself. "It may not be the smoothest whiskey," he said with a laugh, "but it sure as hell gets the job done."

With that he walked, his steps slow and careful, to the house.

"To the fallen!" I cried as he got to the door.

He raised his fist into the air and stumbled into the house.

With Colonel Williams gone, it suddenly seemed cold and the vast sky above us seemed dangerous. Like we were mice that had been enjoying an open plain in daylight before we remembered the eagles. Licia shivered, and I looked up. They were watching us. They were listening to us. They were plotting against us.

I looked at Licia and her face looked stricken. "I'm glad he came," I said. "It's been too long."

Licia nodded, yawned, and grabbed my hand. "Let's go in. I'm cold."

Licia and I didn't sleep much that night. We didn't speak either. We held each other, my mind racing. A new threat, this one from within.

10 / RESISTANCE

THAT DAY IN THE INTERROGATION ROOM I TRIED NOT TO SAY anything. I was feeling so vulnerable from my dream, about not being able to close my eyes and see Licia's face. I knew if I said anything, I'd say everything.

"Did you not sleep well?" the voice asked. It was as smooth as ever, calm and even, entirely in control.

I didn't answer. I didn't want to be here anymore. I needed to get out.

I was starting to hate that smooth voice and I was truly hating the little walks down to this room. I used to like it, any reason to get out of my cell, but they treated me like I was radioactive, and that was wearing on me too.

Yes, I know that I can be literally radioactive, but maybe a better way of saying this is that they were treating me like a leper, like the mere touch of my skin could taint them.

When it was time, three of them came. One with an alien energy weapon, one with a handgun, and one with a long grey metal pole with my handcuffs attached. It's the pole that got to me. They made me go to the back of the cell while they unlocked the cell door. The man with the pole then extended it to me and I had to put my wrists in it. He triggered something on his end and the cuffs snicked into place and I was led that way to interrogation.

Yes, they were afraid of me, I get that. But there was no talking at all. The first time they held up signs for me so I knew what to do. They all looked the same, blank expressions on their faces with dark sunglasses over their eyes. There was no human connection here.

They marched me down to the room, the man holding the pole in front of me walking backwards, the two with the guns behind me.

"We can end this right now. Today," the voice said, interrupting my thoughts. "Tell me the truth, all of it, and we will let you go."

I squeezed my eyes shut tight trying, again, to remember what Licia looked like. I could smell her in my mind, that ozone tang she emits after she's been Lightningirl, I could feel her hand in mine, I could even hear her laughter, but I couldn't see her face.

"You can go back to her," he said. "We don't want to keep you apart, but we need to know everything."

I clenched my fists tight and squeezed my eyes closed tighter.

Why was I resisting? Was it for Tom Tyree the psychopath and his gang of villains? Was it shame for the choices I've made, letting Tom go twice, not going after Chaosboy after he jumped off the roof of the Golden Nugget, failing to stop Gaia at the Hoover Dam?

For a moment I didn't know why I didn't tell them. I didn't understand my resistance. I lifted my head up and looked around the empty room. There was the camera, its big black eye staring at me, but nothing else. Smooth white walls, a single door, nothing else.

"No," I said, the first word I had uttered this time. They had kept me in the dark, they had treated me as a tool, not a person, they threw me in this cell and treated me like a pariah. This wasn't a conversation. This wasn't a partnership.

"Please be reasonable, Nik."

His use of my first name made me madder. We weren't friends —hell, we weren't even acquaintances. I didn't know his name, or what he really looked like. I didn't know how old he was or if he liked baseball or football better. I didn't know if he had kids or if he liked to ride motorcycles.

I slowly stood, my fists clenched, my jaw tight. "Don't call me that."

There was a pause. "What should I call you?"

"I'm done. Take me back to my cell." I could feel my heart pounding and my face flushing red. I was angry and that was enough to keep me from giving away my secrets. But I feared it wouldn't last, that I would grow weak again.

"We are not done here," the smooth voice said.

I walked to the door and tried the shiny silver nob. It was locked.

"Don't do that," he said.

If I just had a knife maybe I could jimmy the lock. I looked around the room, knowing it was silly, but still needing to do something, but there was nothing. The chair in the middle of the room bolted to the floor. The camera mounted on the wall.

"Please sit down."

The chair was metal, the back of it made up of square hollow pieces of metal. Maybe I could break it and jimmy the lock with that.

I walked over to the chair and started kicking the back of it from the side. It was strong and the blows were painful to my foot. The metal on the left side of the seatback bent a little, but it wasn't much.

"You must sit down." The voice was still as calm and even as ever.

I ignored it and kept kicking, switching to my other foot.

"This is your last warning."

I was working up a sweat and it felt good. With each blow I gave a growling grunt of effort, giving voice in a small way to my anger. It was going to give way, eventually. I could see that.

Then there was a strange smell in the air, it had the sweetness of almonds, but was sour too. What is that?

I paused to catch my breath. I was dizzy.

The smell was getting stronger. I didn't like it. My legs gave way and I knew nothing.

11 / BROKEN

"DO YOU FEEL BETTER NOW?" THE VOICE ASKED AS IF FROM very far away. My mouth tasted like greasy metal shavings and my head hurt. I was sitting in the bland interrogation room, sitting in that metal chair, I could feel the damage I did to it, the bent side pressed against my back.

I tried to rub my face, to wake myself up, but I couldn't, my hands were down by my side. They had me handcuffed to the chair, a chain passing under the chair keeping my hands low.

I spit on the clean floor trying to clear that awful taste from my mouth.

"Let's resume where we left off," the smooth voice said. "This Byte woman. You haven't described her to me yet."

That weakness I felt when I woke up from that dream, not being able to see Licia's face, it was gone. I still couldn't see her face, but it wasn't making me weak anymore. It was making me angry. They took me away from her. They locked me up down here. Except for the brief visits from Ronald, they deprived me of the simple comfort of human interaction.

I groaned and strained against my handcuffs feeling them cut into my skin.

"Please don't do that," he said evenly.

I slowed my breathing, taking deep and measured breaths. I knew how to transform into Neutrinoman, it's all about finding that spark and igniting that change. Like a match to kindling.

"What are you doing?" he asked.

I had no charge, no fuel if you will, but I was determined.

"Stop that," he said.

I knew that this is what they feared, and I wanted to give it to them. I had no fuel but my anger and my body. Let it be the fuel. I will change to Neutrinoman. I will fly out of here. I will not listen to that voice one more minute.

"I am afraid that I must insist," he said, his voice still even. "Open your eyes now or I will be forced to take measures."

It's will that does it. Just like I can will my hand into a fist, I can will myself to turn into Neutrinoman. I felt hot and sweat trickled down my back. The voice was still speaking but I didn't hear it. That trigger was there, I knew it was there. My anger was the fuel. I was the fuel. I flipped the switch and...

Nothing.

I slumped in the chair exhausted, defeated, vulnerable.

―――

THERE WAS NOTHING LEFT OF ME AFTER MY FAILURE TO TURN neutrino, handcuffed to that chair. Powerless.

The voice asked more questions, but I wasn't listening. I was falling into a deep, dark pit of despair. It was just me down here. The guards weren't really people. The voice, my interrogator, wasn't either. He was too calm and collected. That voice could be a computer for all the empathy and humanity it contained.

I know the isolation was meant to break me. They had my psych profile. They probably knew my mind better than I did.

They had chosen this isolation purposefully to break me. But they broke me too well.

I chuckled, a brief bitter bark.

"What are you laughing at?" the voice asked.

Tom Tyree and his gang had used my psych profile to manipulate me. First at Yellowstone, tapping into my sense of duty. Then at the LoVE base, presenting me with an open exchange of ideas which I had been longing for.

And what had the military used to manipulate me? My most basic of human needs. My need for human interaction and dignity. They had done something much more villainous than Tom had to me.

Tom had tried to build me into something that could defeat the Aliens. These people had just torn me down. If not for Ronald's brief visits it would have happened much sooner.

And that there, that anomaly, tickled at my brain, but I had no time for it, it was just a whisper against the scream of my despair.

I laughed then. I laughed hard, the sound coming deep from within my belly with a high-pitched manic tang to it.

"Can you please share?" the voice asked.

I laughed until my belly hurt.

"What is so funny?"

"This is working," I began. "This scheme of yours. You are breaking me. You will get what you want this way. Congratulations."

"Why is that funny?" he asked.

"Because of you," I said, "I won't be there to fight if aliens come back. The Earth will fall."

"Let's go back to this Byte woman," he said as if nothing had happened.

I laughed again until my body was too tired to laugh. I knew I sounded crazy, but I didn't care. They eventually uncuffed me from the chair and led me back to my cell.

⊏⊐

"Maybe what you need is something more real," Ronald offered.

"What?" I asked. I had heard him arrive, but hadn't stirred, slumped on my bunk, the scratchy wool blanket underneath me. It wasn't mealtime, it wasn't time for him to be here. Despite the fiction, I had slipped back into that dark place. The place where I didn't believe I'd ever get out. Where I believed I was powerless to change my situation.

"As good as it is, a man can only take so much Jack Reacher." Ronald had a compassionate smile on his face. It was a kind face. A trustworthy face. I didn't trust it.

Keys jangled and I heard the snick of the pass-through door opening and closing.

"Give that a shot," he said.

I levered myself up from my bunk and stumbled over to the pass-through, which was in the wall right next to the door. It had a lockable opening on the outside and it was just big enough for a food tray, wide, but not very high, making it a good size for books. In it was a slim, beat-up book. *A Gradual Awakening* by Stephen Levine. The cover was in sepia tones with a tall spindly tree leaning towards the right and a mountaintop just visible through a misty barrier.

It looked like new-age nonsense to me.

"Why?" I asked him, my face close to the metal bars of my cell.

He licked his lips and looked me up and down. I hadn't showered or shaved in days and I stunk. He looked over his shoulder, as if checking for observers. Which was strange. They were watching, we both knew it.

"Look," he whispered. "I'm not supposed to be giving you any books at all, but this one... you need this one. Just read it."

"They're not going to let me out, are they?" I asked.

Ronald's face darkened and he licked his lips again and sighed.

"In or out, prisoner or free, you need to read that book. You need to get your head in the game."

I snorted and shook my head, "Why?"

His old brown eyes locked with mine. "I believe in you, even if you don't believe in yourself."

With that he turned and walked away.

━━

"Who were you talking to yesterday?" the voice asked. I'm back in the interrogation room, the bent metal of the chair pressed against my back.

"Please no games today," I said, my voice low, my head down. "You know who I was talking to."

A pause. In my mind my interrogator was no longer short and bald. He was tall and handsome with thick black hair. I could see his symmetrical face clearly in my mind, but I still couldn't see Licia's.

"Let's go back to after the breach of the Hoover Dam," the smooth voice said, "when you were talking to Toxicwasteman. What did he tell you?"

"He told me what he always tells me," I said. "That the military, you guys, would screw this up if you were given enough time."

"Can you try to remember the exact words, please?" he said.

"What does it matter?" I asked. "He was right, you know."

"Right about what?" he asked.

"About you screwing this up," I said.

"What have we screwed up?"

I shook my head and got up, started pacing around the room. It was much smaller than my cell, but I felt better moving than I did sitting. I stayed close to the walls. Two and half paces to a side. It seemed to be perfectly square.

"What have we screwed up?" the voice repeated.

I stopped right below the camera. I wasn't sure if it was the only camera in the room, but if it was, this made the conversation more even. I couldn't see him and maybe he couldn't see me.

"The military and I are done," I whispered. I didn't feel strong enough to say it out loud.

"We are not part of the military," the voice said. He said it in his always-even tone, but it made my blood run cold.

"Who are you?" I asked.

"Let's go back to after the breach of the Hoover Dam," he began, but I wasn't listening anymore. If they weren't the military, who were they? CIA? FBI? Homeland Security? It was some sort of governmental organization, wasn't it? It had to be, didn't it?

THE NEXT MORNING—WELL, IT WAS CLOSER TO NOON, WE were all nursing hangovers—we took Colonel Williams for a tour of our little home. He had been here before, but it had been over a year, and we didn't get many visitors, so we probably gave him the kind of in-depth tour that would make most people run for the hills.

We showed him my workshop—really just an oversized shed stuffed with tools—the small greenhouse, and the large greenhouse that we had just completed. The plants were just sprouting and Licia was very proud. She went in depth on each plant, how long they take to mature, how we were going to be able to grow all our own produce.

It was overkill, on both of our parts, but we had gotten so isolated that we needed someone else to talk to. Williams took it in stride, nodding at the right places, asking questions that showed he had been listening. Asking Licia what it would take if he started a small garden, telling her that maybe he needed a hobby other than the brewing of whiskey.

"So what's next?" he asked. "Do you have plans to build something else?"

"A root cellar," I said.

"Really? Why?" he asked.

"The same reason anyone has ever had a root cellar," Licia said, "to keep canned goods cool. With this greenhouse we're going to produce enough food that preserving makes sense."

The truth of the matter was that we could grow produce year-round in the greenhouses. We didn't need a root cellar, what we needed was something to do with our time. But this was a pleasant and civilized conversation, so I kept those thoughts to myself.

"We're currently scouting for a location," I said. "The ground here is full of rocks, so it's not going to be easy."

Williams gave me a raised-eyebrow look. "No powers then?"

I shook my head. "Just us. Just shovels and picks."

He looked like he was pondering the situation. This conversation we were having was a little play for our listeners. Our voices were a bit rough, our words a bit awkward, but that could easily be blamed on the hangovers.

"Well, let's take a look," he said.

We walked the property, showing him the spots we had discussed. Just in back of the house, over by my little workshop, and next to the new greenhouse.

At the last stop he kicked at the ground and then stooped, pulling a beige rock out of the soil. "I wouldn't do it here," he said looking at us, his eyes squinting against the bright sunlight. "Looks like there's more rocks than average."

"I don't know," Licia said. "It's all rocky, and I like the things in orderly lines."

Williams shrugged. "Suit yourself. It's your backs, not mine."

So we had our spot. That night as we sat around the fire under the stars, we had another one of those weird conversations. We spoke of things unimportant and signed of the things most important. We drank wine, Licia insisted, and didn't get nearly as intoxicated, but did drink enough to make our spoken conversation full of laughter.

Next step, Williams signed, *Nik needs to revive his EMV.*

EMV: Electromagnetic Vision. It was a skill I developed while I was being "detained." It requires a half-meditative state and allows me to "see" electromagnetic radiation.

I groaned in response. I never found the skill an easy one to maintain. The mental state can be very frustrating to achieve.

"Oh," Licia said, "looks like you need more wine." She was covering for the groan.

"Yeah, Nichols, it's early. Don't stop now." *It's the only way you'll find the bomb,* he signed.

"If Sunni could see you now," I said.

Williams grinned. "Oh, after fifty years together, I can assure you she knows exactly what I'm up to." *And you must find the bomb. Soon.*

"You should bring her along next time," Licia said.

Williams nodded. *The writing, the interview you agreed to with Diane Madison, some people are getting very nervous. So dig and quick.*

13 / THE PRISON INSIDE

THE BOOK RONALD LEFT ME WAS BORING AND HARD TO READ.
A book on vipassana meditation. The reasons, whys, and tech-
niques. I longed for a better escape, one with heroes and heroines.
One with action and adventure.

And that was sad. I wasn't longing to physically escape from
these four walls but to mentally escape, what I wanted right then
was some good fiction with some action and adventure. I could no
longer imagine physical escape.

I don't know that I really identify with being a "hero." I find the
word to be troublesome. I mean, in fiction I know what it is, but not
in the real world. The real world is a lot messier and a lot more
complicated. Someone looking at my actions and not living through
them with all the doubts and second-guessing might use that word,
but I wouldn't.

Lee Child's Jack Reacher was very much on my mind. Highly
skilled and capable, Reacher only got involved when he had to,
when things got too close to him personally. When there was no
other choice.

He seemed more of an anti-hero to me, and that was appealing. He just wanted everyone to leave him alone. He just wanted to wander. And right about then, that sounded perfect to me, provided Licia was along for the wandering.

But I didn't have a Jack Reacher novel and boredom did its job and I would pick up the meditation book and read a little, it's words mostly bouncing off me, mostly making no sense. And then I would pace until I couldn't stand it anymore and then flop down into my bunk and read a little more.

In fits and starts, I read that book about the nature of the human mind written by an American Buddhist. How the real prison we all face is inside our own minds, not in our circumstances. A treatise, if you will, on the care and tending of the human mind.

I didn't buy it at first. I was a hot dog and football kind of a guy, an "I'll believe it when I see it" person. Just a nobody drifting through my life until the accident at the Palo Verde Nuclear Generating Station. But that book was the only one I had. Ronald had taken the Jack Reacher novels back when I was done with them. What else was I going to do?

The foreword and introduction threw me off. They seemed too full of words that didn't make sense to me and written decades ago from a perspective so foreign. But then I hit the last sentence of the first paragraph of the first chapter: "Meditation *is* awareness."

After the accident and the cosmic rays, after I got these powers, I had to learn to understand my body and what I was feeling. I had taken up long-distance running which can be meditative, very meditative if you let it. I didn't have a word for it before, but awareness was something I had been cultivating, something I needed to be Neutrinoman. Awareness of my flesh and blood body and awareness of my q-morph form. I was locked in a cell and the idea of becoming more aware was appealing—given, of course, that I had no fiction to read.

So I read. In fits and starts. Rereading, sometimes over and over. Learning about vipassana meditation and how the mind works. Wondering if this would help.

Eventually, I found the exact center of my cell—a little OCD, I will admit—took the thin, scratchy blanket off my bunk, folded it up, and sat there. I felt silly knowing I was being watched, knowing my every move was being evaluated.

I just sat there and paid attention to my breathing, feeling the stale air flow in and out of my nostrils, my eyes half closed, listening to my mind rebel.

This is stupid. How is sitting here going to help me? It's not. Sitting isn't going to get me out of here. I have to find a way to become Neutrinoman and blast my way out or I need to tell them everything and get this over with.

I made it maybe thirty seconds that first time. But really, all I had there was time. So I would go back to my bunk, read a little more, and then go back to the center of the cell and sit there cross-legged listening to my mind babble on.

Quinn is out there with Licia. He's pretending to be you. She may have decided she likes him better than you by now. You can't even remember what she looks like, you...

That wasn't even fifteen seconds. That voice was the one that hurt. It spoke in my mind like it wasn't me, like it was outside of me, like it knew things I didn't.

This time I didn't go back to the book, I started pacing. I needed out of this cell. I needed human contact. I needed Licia.

"How's it going?" Ronald asked from the bars of my cell. I hadn't heard him walk up.

"I hate that book," I snapped.

Ronald smiled. "Then it's doing its job."

I walked to the bars. Ronald smelled of Old Spice, which made me think of my father. "What do you mean?"

"Well, the novels help you escape out of yourself, provide some relief," he said.

I nodded.

"This one asks you to go into yourself, to confront the demons there, to understand how your mind really works. Not fun, but more useful in your particular circumstance."

He just stood there, a bemused smile on his old face. I didn't want to confront my inner demons. I just wanted the hell out of here. "I don't think I can do this much longer."

His eyebrows furrowed, and I swear his eyes misted up. "Keep practicing. If you do, I'll bring you another Reacher book tomorrow."

SUMMER 2005, LOCATION UNKNOWN

"What are you reading now?" the voice asked as I slumped in that metal chair in the middle of that square room with white walls.

What I wouldn't give for a piece of art hanging on the wall. A landscape... hell, give me a finger painting by a five-year-old at this point and I would be happy. Something to look at. Something with life. Something with character.

"What puzzles me," I said, "is why you want me to read it."

"What do you mean?" he asked.

"You control everything here, including Ronald. Why did you send him down with that book? It doesn't make sense." I was having trouble reconciling Ronald and the positive effect he was having on me with the aims of the people that imprisoned me.

"Why do you think we did it?" the smooth voice asked.

"No," I said, standing up from the metal chair and going into the corner of the room without the camera. "None of the psychological mumbo-jumbo. Either answer the question or don't."

There was a lengthy pause. "What does Ronald look like?"

The room felt small to me, like the walls were closing in. Why the hell would they ask a question like that unless they were messing with me?

"What does Ronald look like?" the voice repeated with the exact same inflection and intonation.

"Bald. Old. Black... Why are you asking me this? You know what he looks like."

Another long pause. "Tell me about the book Ronald gave you."

I slid down to the floor, my back pressed against the wall, my breathing rapid, sweat pricking out on the back of my neck and my arm pits.

"What is the title of the book?" my interrogator asked.

Why were they asking me questions they knew the answer to? The room seemed smaller, the walls against my back hard and cool, the hum of the air blowing into the room loud.

"It's a simple question, you know," he said.

"What? What is?" I asked.

"What is the title of the book?"

I didn't answer, but slowly rose, my back pressed firmly into the corner. My heart was thudding in my chest, my face flushed. I reached up above me to the camera. It was small, mounted on a little metal bracket, just barely within my reach standing on my tiptoes.

I moved slowly, feeling for screws or another way to release it. I wasn't really thinking this through, I was just acting. I needed to escape the voice, the endless questions. The questions that he had to know the answers to.

As I was feeling around, I felt the two wires connected to the camera. One for power, one for the video feed. Electricity! My fingers were hungry. My cells had none, but this room did. I blinked and looked around the room carefully studying the walls. It was a foolish hope, but I was looking to see if there was a power outlet in the room.

Of course there wasn't.

"What is the title of the book?" he asked, his tone infuriatingly even.

Sweat was trickling down my back. How could I get the wires off quickly? Could I get enough electricity to change before they gassed me?

I should take my time, think about it, study the connections. But I didn't have enough will to wait. I jumped up with a grunt, got my hands fully around the little camera and pulled hard.

With a snap it came off the wall, the wires snaking out of their holes a bit. I yanked and the camera came loose from the wires and I let it drop to the floor.

The voice didn't speak, but I started to smell sour almonds again. I took a deep breath and held it, turning around and looking at the wires.

Both of them had copper exposed. Neither of them were large, not like a normal power plug. They didn't come very far out of the wall so I had to reach up to grab them. I pressed my fingers against the copper conductors.

I could feel it. Sweet electricity. Not much, it was low power and definitely DC, but it was electricity nonetheless. I almost shouted out in joy, but kept my mouth closed, holding my breath.

I willed the change, tried to flip the switch, as soon as the meager current started flowing through my veins. This was no power-up from Lightningirl—it was the drip-drip of a leaky faucet, where she was the roar of Niagara Falls.

It wasn't enough, but I tried anyway. I let the electricity flow through me while my lungs screamed for oxygen, while the voice—still maddeningly steady—asked me what I was doing, while the beefy boys in black busted into the room wearing gas masks and started shooting me with the alien energy weapons. Still I stood there, ignoring it all. The purple balls of energy didn't really do anything to me—I had no power to rob.

I twisted around, still holding the wires so I could see them.

Three men, one with the alien energy weapon—the silver tube and awkward backpack—and two with handguns.

"Step away from the wires," one of the men said, his voice muffled because of the gas mask. He raised his gun and pointed it at me. His voice was rough and he sounded scared and had a bit of a southern drawl. Not the voice of my interrogator. "Do it now or I will shoot."

I smiled. One of the guards had spoken to me. It was a tiny victory, but a victory nonetheless. They had left the door open and the smell of almonds was dissipating. I took a few breaths and felt lightheaded but it wasn't enough to knock me out. "No," I said, my voice as calm as my interrogator.

He took a step forward and cocked back the hammer on the gun. "I will shoot you."

"No you won't," I said. I didn't really believe what I was saying, but I wanted to. The way they had treated me was all about breaking my will but keeping me alive.

He pulled his gas mask off, the muscles of his jaw bunched and his green eyes connected with mine briefly, but then flicked away. I studied him. He had loose black pants on, a black long-sleeved shirt, with a black multi-pocket vest. On his belt was the holster for his gun, a walkie-talkie, and a Taser.

I almost cried out in joy. A Taser. Not much amperage, but 50,000 volts. That could do it. I had trouble making my eyes leave his belt and return to his face. I wanted that Taser like a drunk wants his first drink of the day.

Another thought occurred to me seeing that Taser. I'm not the only prisoner. If I was, they wouldn't have those. It's too dangerous to have them around me.

"Step away, right now." He lowered his gun, pointing it at my leg. He wasn't going to try to kill me, but he was willing to shoot me.

I took a deep breath and nodded slowly but didn't let go of the electricity yet. It wasn't much, just a few crumbs to a starving man. But it was something.

"What's your name?" I asked. "Tell me your name and I'll let go."

He blinked and looked up and to the right. He was going over his orders in his head. Knowing that he wasn't supposed to interact with me at all. But maybe preserving my life was a higher priority.

"Evan," he said as if revealing a secret. "Evan Saunders."

I still held onto the wire. "You married or got a girlfriend? Any kids?" Evan was about 5'10" and strong with black hair, a square jaw, and pale green eyes. He was somewhere in his early thirties.

"Let go of the wires," he said. "Now!"

I bit my lip, hard. I had made a deal and it was hard to not do it. To not let go like I had said I was. "Just answer that question. I'll let go then. I promise."

"I had a girl but then I went to Iraq," he said, his voice even, but his eyes flicking around. "She didn't wait for me."

I almost smiled. Not because of his sad story, but because he was human. I was so relieved. He wasn't just a square-jawed beefy boy anymore. He was Evan Saunders with green eyes, the Iraq vet that missed his girl.

"Sorry about that, Evan," I said as I lowered my hands.

He gave me a sharp nod as he backed up. One of the other guards backed out of the room and came back with the long pole with the handcuffs on it. Evan held his gun on me while the other guard pointed the alien energy weapon at me. The third guard held the pole and got close enough so it was right in front of me.

"No," I said, looking from the handcuffs to Evan. "I think I know my way back to my cell by now."

"You have to," Evan said.

"I don't think I do," I said.

Evan held his finger to his ear and I noticed a black earbud in there. A thin wire snaked down to his walkie-talkie. He was receiving orders. "Very well," he said. "Let's go."

15 / YOU MUST SURVIVE

SUMMER 2025, CASITA DE SOLEDAD, CENTRAL ARIZONA

WILLIAMS STAYED TWO MORE NIGHTS. EACH NIGHT WE drank. Each night we signed. On our flagstone patio under the bright stars, our isolated high-desert home feeling less and less safe.

He made it clear to us that Project Vulcan was in place, that the powers that be were nervous about our current activity. He didn't know exactly what should be done, but he said that we needed to get to the bomb and do "something" about it.

That something was what was at question. Disarming it made sense, but I was no bomb expert. And could I really spend time on the internet learning about them? Wouldn't our guards figure that out? They listened to us, they watched us, surely they monitored our digital activity.

During those next two days we dug. Williams volunteered for the hard duty of helping us break ground. He grumbled and complained about the location, told us we should move it—again playing his part for our audience—but he swung a pick and wielded a shovel. He wasn't fast, but he was steady. Damn impressive for his age.

That last night, Licia brought up what I didn't want to talk about. We were back to Williams's Whiskey (as we had come to call it). Our mood was somber. We were physically tired, and for my part I wasn't ready to see him go. It had been nice to have company.

We were out on the patio, a fire blazing, and for once we weren't talking (verbally) very much.

What if we stop? No writing. No interviews, Licia signed.

I shot back some whiskey and grimaced. I didn't know if that was a life I could go back to.

Williams looked at me, a grim smile on his angular face. He rubbed at his brush-cut, a gesture so old and so familiar it made me smile despite myself. *Let's face facts*, he signed. *He's not going to do that, so I didn't bring it up.*

Licia looked at me, her brown eyes hard. She didn't need to sign. The question was obvious.

He's right, I signed.

"The smoke's a little much," Licia said, getting up. "I'm going to get some air." She walked quickly away towards the site of our excavation.

A noisy sigh escaped my lips.

"Glass is empty, I see," Williams said, refiling it.

It's too much, I signed.

That it is, he signed back.

What do I do?

You must survive, he signed. *The world may need you again.*

I groaned noisily and got up, those words curdling into something sour in my stomach. I was sick of people needing me to survive. I was sickened by being thought of as a savior, a hero. I know we would have failed without Colonel Williams and so many others, I just happened to be the one with some raw power. I couldn't stand the thought of anyone else sacrificing themselves for me, too many had already.

"I'm going to go check on Licia," I mumbled. I left Williams there and walked out into the night. The moon wasn't up yet and it was dark, the stars bright pinpricks of light above. I couldn't see very well, but I knew the way. I smelled her before I saw her. Alcohol mingled with sweat and the sour smell of fear. She hadn't been Lightningirl for a while so the ozone scent of her was missing.

My eyes were adjusting and I found Licia at our excavation site. It wasn't much yet, just a rectangle about eight feet on a side and two feet deep. We had a long way to go. My muscles ached from the digging, but it was a good ache.

I walked up next to her and just stood there. We needed to talk, to have the kind of long conversations we had had so many times in our relationship. The kind that starts on one topic and meanders for hours, that goes around and around a problem until you can finally see it, can finally talk about it. The kind of insight that can only come from a long talk with someone you love.

But we couldn't do that. We now knew we were being watched, recorded, and evaluated. 24/7. That we had no privacy. That this beautiful home we had built was just as much a prison as that twelve-by-twelve cell that they had thrown me in after the Hoover Dam incident.

Licia slipped her hand into mine and squeezed it hard.

"I love you," I said, hoping that those three words conveyed what I needed them to. That I was sorry that I had gotten us into this mess but didn't know what else to do. I've had my freedom taken away before and I couldn't keep living this way.

"I love you too," she said, her voice low and rough.

"I... I've been thinking about that Diane Madison interview," I said. It was a risk to say anything directly, but I had to say something. "Maybe we shouldn't. She's not the most trustworthy woman."

Licia snorted. "No argument there. But I disagree. We should do it. We need to get out of our shell here a little." She squeezed my hand hard again. She was telling me it was okay, that we would figure it out.

Without a word we walked hand and hand back to Colonel Williams. We made good use of his whiskey, our laughter ringing out into the night, and sent him off in style.

16 / HUMANIZING FACTORS

"CAN YOU TELL ME ANYTHING ELSE ABOUT EVAN SAUNDERS?"
I asked Ronald. He had asked me about the meditation work, but I
was done with letting everyone else set the direction down here.

"Evan?" he asked, his wrinkled face putting on an impressive
show through the bars as his forehead furrowed.

I nodded. "He's one of the guards. We met during yesterday's
little incident."

Ronald looked briefly puzzled, like he didn't know what I was
talking about. Then his face relaxed and he said, "With the
camera?" he asked.

"How many exciting things happen down here every day?"

He chuckled. "Not many."

"So, what do you know about him?" I asked.

Ronald shrugged. "He's a soldier, follows orders, is from the
south, loves soccer."

I nodded and smiled. It wasn't much, but a tiny bit more about
Evan, making him a tiny bit more human.

"And the meditations?" Ronald asked.

"They suck," I said. And they did. The book talked about how you could get to this point where the mind shut up, but I hadn't. This morning's attempts were filled with remembering the incident in interrogation and wondering about Evan.

"Good," Ronald said and turned to go.

"You got a girl, Ronald?" It was the same question I had asked Evan, but Ronald's age made it sound a little awkward.

He turned, one eyebrow raised, his hand rubbing at his bald head.

"Or a guy, for that matter," I added. "Do you have somebody?"

He smiled, but it was bitter and wistful, his dark eyes darting away from mine. "She died."

"I'm sorry," I said.

I could see the emotions playing across his face. Pain, regret, grief. It was like looking at the foamy chop of a big lake on a windy day. I knew there was a lot more below the surface.

I felt for him, missing Licia as I was, but the added evidence of humanity down in this hole was uplifting.

"Maybe you need to meditate," I offered.

He chuckled and with a wave left me.

I went back to the wool blanket in the middle of my cell, crossed my legs, and tried to center myself.

⸻

It happened slowly. At first, I wasn't aware it was happening, that time had slipped by in the oddest way. I'd be sitting there on that scratchy wool blanket in the middle of my cell fighting to stay present with my breath, to note my thoughts and just let them go, and suddenly it would be later in the day.

No clock down there. No real sense of day or night except the light being on or off. It was my stomach that was my best guide to time. And my little meditations would last longer without seeming longer, my stomach clock told me the truth.

At first it was so subtle that I didn't notice. But then it became obvious. Dinner was coming much sooner than I thought it should (but not my stomach).

The meditations still sucked, my thoughts still ran around my head holding riots of guilt, grief, and condemnation. But time started to slip by more smoothly.

And when you are stuck in a cell with no one to talk to, that is a wonderful thing.

"You seem happy today," Ronald said after I had been trying my meditations for a month, maybe longer. I couldn't track the days very well either. I was pretty sure another season had passed outside while I sat in this cell learning about my mind. Summer to fall, and while part of me despaired that I would never leave, none of that mattered for those precious moments when I could really meditate.

I shrugged. I didn't feel happy. I had all the same problems. But I did feel a little lighter. As if the burden of the loneliness and isolation weren't so bad.

"Got a Grisham for you today," he said, putting a book in the pass-through. "*A Time to Kill*. It's his first novel."

"Thanks, Ronald. You're a good man."

Ronald did a half-snort that sounded like he doubted my declaration.

"You are," I insisted. I had noticed that he took back all the fiction I had been reading until I really started to meditate, then he would let me keep a few of my favorites. When he wanted me to meditate, he gave me nothing else to read. His ability to get me to do something good for myself made him the best kind of man.

Ronald gave me a weary smile on his aged face. "Don't know about that, but thanks."

"What do you mean?" I asked.

He stepped right up to the bars, his brown eyes locking with mine. I was standing in my cell a few feet back. He was my height so our eyes lined right up. "If I was such a good man, I wouldn't be stuck down here with you."

I stepped close and whispered, "Are there other prisoners down here." The Tasers the guards wore seemed to indicate there were.

His head bobbed up and down just the tiniest bit as he said, "Just you. All of this for you."

He turned and walked away.

"Why do they let you talk to me?" I called after him. It didn't make sense. It bugged me constantly. Our brief conversations and the books he brought me were lending me strength. They were helping me keep my secrets. Why would they do that?

Ronald didn't answer, he just held his hand up and waved without looking back.

INTERROGATION TIME CHANGED AFTER THE INCIDENT WITH the camera. I would no longer wear the cuffs. This resulted in interrogation not happening for a few days. Evan Saunders and the other two guards had come for me as usual. Evan with a gun, another guard with the alien energy weapon, and the third with the handcuff pole.

"No," I said, looking at Evan. He had his dark sunglasses back on, his lips a tight thin line. "I'll go, but no cuffs."

They didn't speak, but when it was clear I wasn't going to cooperate, they left and didn't come back the next day.

When they did come back, Evan held up a sign at my refusal that said, "Cooperate or we will force you."

"Go ahead," I said.

They quickly departed. That night they didn't bring dinner and Ronald didn't show up. Punishment. I just meditated more.

The next day the same routine. I said no and they didn't feed me. And the next and the next.

The first two days, the constant gnawing in my stomach was

loud and unbearable. It just wouldn't shut up. Hungry. Hungry. Hungry. It's like my mind was a skipping record.

I took that into meditation and let it get as loud as it wanted. *We're going to die. We have to have food. Just put the cuffs on and they'll feed you.* On and on it went in endless variety. I just kept focusing on my breath, my eyes half slits gazing at the floor and the bars of my cell, noting the thoughts of hunger and letting them go.

I had meditated enough now to understand that most of my thoughts were boring and repetitive. I was still having the same thoughts I did before I started meditating, but I was taking them a lot less seriously. The good thoughts, the bad thoughts, and all the ones in between.

On the third day of this, I started to feel a lightness to my body and the hunger pangs stopped. I was surprised at first, I didn't expect it to feel good. The layer of belly fat that I still had was melting away—which was fine with me—but I knew that once the fat was gone this was going to start to get serious.

So I wasn't hungry physically, but I was worried.

I sat crossed-legged on that wool blanket and let those fears bounce around my head, just observing them as dispassionately as I could and coming back to my breath, my gaze soft, what I could see of my tiny cell, the bars, and the hallway blurry through my eyelashes.

I guess I could have stared at the wall, not had the bars of my cell in my field of view, but the cell door was the way out of here—it symbolized freedom.

No food. No Ronald. No voices but my own.

It drove me to meditate more and more. To seek solace in that still space between breaths.

The change, when it came, wasn't a lot, it wasn't like I suddenly felt a bolt of lightning come down from the sky and I suddenly knew everything. It was subtle, like every time I sat, every time I could endure my mind's jabbering, I would feel just a little lighter. Just a little bit better.

It didn't change my situation, it just made it bearable.

And fasting helped. A lot. My body wasn't digesting food anymore, and while I knew it would kill me long-term, short-term it just powered that sense of lightness.

I didn't care if Ronald came or if I got to talk to someone even if it was that bland voice of my interrogator. It didn't matter. I had my wool blanket. I had my breath. It was all I needed.

On the fifth day of my fast is when it happened. The guards had left, me having refused the cuffs yet again, and I sat down to meditate, knowing it would be another long day of isolation.

It was subtle at first. My eyes were a bit more open than usual, wanting to see more of the hallway and what it symbolized. I was staring at the wall at the end of the hallway where it turned to the right. There was a one-way mirror there and I knew there was a guard back there with an alien energy weapon.

When it happened, I could see something beyond the reflection of the mirror. I thought I could see that guard. Kind of.

He was in a sitting position, his body slumped forward, staring right at me.

I didn't think much about it. That meditative state is not about thinking. I just took another breath and watched. I was sure I was imagining it.

The figure I saw was just a ghostly outline in neon blue. He rocked back, rubbed at his face, and then leaned forward again. I hadn't thought much about my guards, about how boring it must be for them watching me all day long just in case I do something.

I let that thought go and went back to my breath. The guard resolved in more details. A neon-blue nimbus around him with thin veins of pulsing blue running through his body, a tight, bright nest of it in his head.

I took a deep breath and let out a long sigh. If I hadn't been so deep in my meditation, I would have questioned what I was seeing. I would have doubted myself. Well, I did doubt myself, and was fascinated by that too. But I just kept letting all those thoughts go.

They were just brief flickerings of the mind. I went back to the breath and kept meditating.

I don't know how long that meditation lasted. I was amused by what I had seen, but wasn't taking it seriously, wasn't seeing the possibilities. Yet.

<hr />

ELECTROMAGNETIC ENERGY. IT'S WHAT LIGHTNINGIRL wields. It's what she can use to charge me when the neutron blast of an atomic reaction isn't available.

But it's all radiation. Electromagnetic radiation. Neutronic radiation. It's what I need to become Neutrinoman.

My fast lasted a total of ten days. During that time I lost about fifteen pounds and became as weak as a kitten. As I became weaker, I just meditated more. As I meditated more, I began to see more.

Ghostly blue lines snaking along the long hallway towards my cell. My guard behind the one-way mirror, a tracery of delicate blue lines with a blue nimbus around him, and a bright purple blotch of energy next to the guard representing the alien energy weapon, a thick pulsing blue line leading to it—they had figured a way to charge them up.

Pale blue auras around Evan Saunders and the other two guards, a bright blue splotch at their belts where their Tasers sat.

It was day ten of the fast and I sat on my wool blanket, my body weak but my sight strong. Evan had a grim look on his face. Evan, who likes soccer not football, who had a girl but she didn't wait for him while he was in Iraq. I thought these thoughts whenever I saw him. It gave me some small measure of comfort.

I let my soft, meditative gaze linger on him. I could see more than just the aura. I could see the tangle of blue in his head, and thin blue lines tracing their way throughout his body.

He unlocked the cell door, his gun trained on me the whole

time. One of the guards stepped forward holding the metal pole with the cuffs on the end. I just shook my head.

"Please," Evan whispered.

I looked at his eyes, but they were hidden behind the dark sunglasses. But no, I could see them now. Light blue orbs of energy, electromagnetic radiation, behind the plastic. I could see all of him. The bright blue of his pulsing heart, the solid blue trunk of his spinal column, nerve impulses racing back and forth, the dense, tangled blue of his mind.

I smiled. Electromagnetic radiation. He and the other guards were biological generators of this energy. I was a biological generator of it too. I looked down at my hand and saw the same delicate trace work of blue lines running through it and I laughed.

It all seemed so simple. I didn't need an external source of power to transform myself to Neutrinoman. I was that source of power. My body turned biological matter into electrical impulses to power my nervous system. It wasn't much power, but I figured it had to be more power than that damn camera I had tried to tap into.

"You've got to," Evan whispered.

I looked up, he was in the cell only a few feet away, the guard with the pole having backed off. His mouth was pulled down into a frown, his forehead creased, his gun lowered. He was worried about me. He was risking backlash by even talking to me. His voice had the slightest hint of a southern twang.

"Where are you from?" I asked, staring past the sunglasses into the blue tracery I could now see that were his eyes.

"They won't feed you until you collapse," he said. "Please, just let us cuff you and then they'll let us feed you."

Was I just being a stubborn fool? Was this line I had drawn an important one? In my starved and meditative state, such questions didn't mean much to me.

"Georgia, maybe," I said, trying to figure out where he was from. "Or South Carolina."

"North Carolina," he said.

I nodded knowingly, like he had just told me something epically important. "You like soccer," I said, "not football."

His brow furrowed. "How do you know that?"

"Ronald told me," I said.

"Who's Ronald?" he asked.

"He brings me books. Talks to me." I smiled broadly at Evan. At this point what we were having seemed like a good long conversation.

My mind slipped back to powering my transformation to Neutrinoman. I was weak, but still electricity flowed through my nervous system. Electromagnetic radiation emanated from Evan and the other guards, from the lights above. It seeped out of the power lines embedded in the walls. It was everywhere.

And then I found it.

"You better take a step back," I said to Evan.

"Why?" he asked.

"I don't want to hurt you," I said calmly.

He slowly rose, his gun trained on me as he stepped out of the cell.

I took it all in. The blue lines of electromagnetic radiation everywhere. Delicate lines running through the bodies of the guards. Bright balls of it where their Tasers were. A purple blob of it on the back of the guard with the alien energy weapon.

They look scared. I didn't blame them.

"Relax, boys," I said. "I'm not going to go anywhere, just going to prove a point."

I took a deep breath. I reached deep for that place within me. The trigger that turned me to Neutrinoman. I flipped the switch and...

And everything went black.

INTERLUDE 1: THE PAST

I have found that taking a long look at one's own past is not a comfortable thing. At least not for me. We tend to see our failures clearly and our successes, while seen, aren't dwelled on. Probably human nature, but this process is not comfortable.

I don't look back on my prison time fondly, but I managed to stumble into some things that proved to be very important. But it's the stumbling, fumbling nature of my performance here in the prison, and really throughout this story, that is becoming hard to watch. It's one thing to know I was faking it all those years, it's entirely another to record it in minute detail.

And sitting here typing away, having the perspective of time and not being in that difficult situation, I find myself having less compassion for the 2005 me than I probably should.

Couldn't I have just transformed into Neutrinoman my first day and flew out? Couldn't I have resisted my interrogator, not let that way-the-hell-too-steady voice get into my head? Couldn't I have been stronger?

Hindsight isn't really 20/20, is it? Twenty years later I am looking at my past as realistically as I can, but I am not that struggling young man that I was then.

Licia, who has a bad habit of reading over my shoulder when I write, just said, "No, dear, you're a struggling older man," with a merry laugh.

While I can see more clearly what was happening, what is less clear is who I was.

I think what I am trying to say is that while time has given me the distance of perspective, it has also dulled the empathy I used to have for that me.

Maybe the same is true for you as you reflect on your past. And I've been doing so much of it I have a bit of advice, if you will indulge me. Be gentle with yourself. You were doing the best you could no matter what it looks like now.

I was doing the best I could back then. I know that. I still wish I had done better.

But, frankly, here in 2025 things are anything but stable for Licia and I, so one kind of danger is past, but another kind is on us. I sit here typing away at my wife's insistence so I hopefully get my head on so we can take on this new challenge, find a new life. Again.

I need to take my own advice and be gentle with myself, I just don't know if we have that luxury.

FALL 2005, LOCATION UNKNOWN

I SAW HIM THROUGH THE WALLS FIRST, THAT BRIGHT BLUE trace work that is the electromagnetic radiation of a human body. The room I had awakened in wasn't my cell. It was a small room with two beds, white cabinets, a sink, and bright fluorescent lights. The infirmary.

I was strapped to one of the beds, an IV slowly dripping fluids into me. I couldn't move much, but I didn't care. I felt energy returning to my starved body. I could see the blue. A halo around the lights, a blue line leading through the ceiling to them.

I turned my head as much as I could to the closed door of the room. I could see the line of blue that brought electricity to the room, the lines of it snaking to the two cameras mounted at two corners of the room. Outside the room, on the other side of the door stood a guard. I could tell because of the ball of blue at his side, a Taser.

And I saw my visitor approaching before I heard his steps or saw the doorknob turn. He was tall and slim without a Taser at his side, so I didn't think he was a guard.

"And how are we feeling?" he said as he entered the room. His voice smooth and even and so very familiar to me. The voice of my interrogator.

He was tall, with sharp cheekbones, green eyes, and grey hair. He wore a white coat, like a doctor, over a white shirt and blue tie. He was neither the short bald man nor the smiling handsome man I had imagined him to be.

"Weak," I answered as I studied him. I still had the sight so it was a bit strange looking at him. The blue lines everywhere, the aura around him.

"Not to worry. You'll be feeling better soon." He was fitting a blood pressure cuff around my arm.

I felt my cheeks flush as I watched him. He wasn't a handsome man or an ugly one, just a regular person, if a bit older than I imagined. But I was mad. He was the one that had asked me all those questions. He was the one that seemed to be in charge. He was the one that had done this to me.

As my anger grew, the blue lines faded away and my vision returned to normal. My state was anything but meditative.

"Are you the one who decided to withhold the food?" I asked. "To do this to me?"

He pulled the blood pressure cuff off, his green eyes connecting with mine. I saw what looked like compassion on his face, but I didn't believe it. "I am," he said with a nod. "I am in charge down here, so it all falls to me." His shoulders slumped as if demonstrating the weight of his burden.

"Why?" I asked.

He sighed and pulled up a stool, slumping down onto it. "You were not cooperating. We needed you to cooperate." He said it as if it were as simple as a math equation. One plus one equals two. You don't cooperate, we withhold food.

"Needed?" I asked, noticing his use of the past tense.

He nodded. "We're releasing you as soon as you are well enough to travel."

I blinked and stared at him, imagining something much worse than this coming next. "Why?"

He smiled, but it was a bitter thing. "The military needs you back in action. From what I've heard there's been some 'chatter' that is disturbing them. For my own part, I believe we were very close to a breakthrough, but..."

"But what?" I asked.

He smiled again, but this time it looked wistful. "Well... This Ronald thing has gotten to be quite disturbing." His tone was still as even as ever, but his mouth puckered into a frown.

"What about Ronald?" I asked. "You sent him to me."

He looked away and shook his head. "I'm afraid that we didn't."

"What?" Ronald with his calming, elegant presence. Ronald who brought me novel after novel and that meditation book. Ronald who would make eye contact with me and talk to me. Ronald who made my stay bearable. It made no sense. "Who sent him?" I asked.

He leaned close, his tone low as if sharing a secret. "I'm sorry to tell you this, but there is no Ronald."

19 / THE BOMB

AFTER COLONEL WILLIAMS LEFT US, LIFE AT CASITA DE Soledad became somewhat stilted. Licia and I dug during the day, slept at night, attended to the plants and the many other things that you have to do when you live off of the grid. We didn't talk much, not about important things. We tried to keep up our normal banter but soon let that go as our fatigue from digging built up. We figured that would be enough cover for our watchers.

At first, under the stars at night, we would sign like we did with Colonel Williams, but soon we stopped doing that. There was nothing left to say. We were in an untenable situation and we didn't know how to get out of it.

So we dug our root cellar, the threat from Project Vulcan looming, and I did my best to reestablish my meditation practice.

Meditation is something that can be wonderful and amazing, but it has its price. You might not think so, I mean, you're just sitting there breathing, how hard can that be? Well, in this case, very hard. Meditation makes you confront yourself, your doubts and your fears.

And I had a lot of them out there in the high desert of central Arizona. I half expected them to trigger the bomb just because we were close. I began to have trouble sleeping, afraid that they would wait until they knew we were asleep and we were vulnerable and then just trigger it.

Boom! No more Neutrinoman and Lightningirl. No more powerful superheroes that are hard to control.

But I kept at it. I kept digging. I kept meditating. Until it was enough.

When the sight came, I was actually digging. Weeks had passed and the hole was six feet deep. I was working with a pick and shovel, filling a bucket, and Licia was raising it up out of the hole and disposing of it.

Physical labor can be meditative if you let it. Your breath becomes important, the stress to your body makes you let go of most of the babble of your thoughts—they're just not important—and you are just *there*.

I had slipped into it rather on accident. One of the basic tenets of meditation is that you don't chase thoughts away, you just know they are going to come up and you let them go. And that is what I had been doing for hours as I dug and Licia hauled. Just the effort and the rhythm of it, the heat and the work, time slipping away without me being very aware of it.

And then I saw it. A dim glimmer of purple far below me. It was small in my sight, but I could see its power. A purple ball of contained energy, waiting to be released.

I had thoughts about it. How far is it? Can I even dig that far? They'll know if I'm getting close. But I went back to my breath and let those thoughts go. I kept digging. I kept looking, as I moved around the pit, and I got a better idea of the bomb's location. We were off a bit. It looked to be about ten feet north of the pit and about fifty feet down.

Later I created a fire out on the patio and Licia and I signed under the moonlight, the cooling air a comfort after a long, hot day.

I told her I had found it and where it was.

What now? she signed.

I shook my head. *We can't dig that far by hand.*

You could get there quickly as Neutrinoman, she signed.

They would know. They would trigger it, I signed.

You could survive it.

I shrugged.

In the flickering yellow firelight, her face fell. I could relate, my stomach was rebelling against our dinner. I think maybe I had held out hope that Williams had been wrong. That Project Vulcan wasn't real, that our watchers wouldn't be willing to sacrifice us if we got far enough out of line.

All that time in prison sitting in that room being asked questions by my faceless interrogator came tumbling back on me. I wasn't isolated here like I was there, but it was similar.

I can't live this way, I signed.

She nodded, her lips a thin line, her face grim.

I stood up and pulled her close, hugging her fiercely.

"You need to leave," I whispered in her ear. "Zap out of here now."

She pushed away far enough to look in my eyes. I don't know what she saw, but her own eyes widened and her mouth opened. "Don't do anything stupid," she whispered.

"I can't live this way," I said.

"And I can't lose you," she replied.

That stopped me short. I was willing to risk my own life, but not hers.

"I'm not leaving," she added. "Whatever we do, we do together."

I nodded and took her hand, leading her through the moonlight towards the power lines. She squeezed my hand hard. We had done this before, gone into battle together, faced our enemies side by side, not knowing if we would survive.

We would live or we would die, but we would do it together.

When we got close to the power lines, we both transformed without a word. She extended her left hand, pulling a crackling bolt of lightning from the high-tension power lines, the energy flowing through her right hand into me, lighting up the night, throwing eerie shadows out across the desert.

"How much do you want?" she shouted.

"As much as you can give me!" I replied. "We're going to dig that thing up. One way or another this will be over tonight."

THERE IS NO RONALD. STRAPPED TO THAT BED IN THE Q-morph prison infirmary, thoughts swirled through my head as fast as a tornado, whipping by at fierce speeds only to be quickly replaced by another thought. But there was a monotony to those thoughts, a uniformity that resolved into one thing: I am crazy.

My interrogator had explained in his calm voice that there was no one named Ronald down here. That they didn't employ an older black man. That they had been disturbed by all the conversations I had had with my "imaginary friend."

I didn't believe him. I got angrier until he grabbed a laptop and started showing me footage of me in my cell.

As the footage played, I'm slumped on my bunk and look up surprised and said, "Who are you?"

The camera changed to one from the back of the cell clearly showing me and the bars of my cell. I was alone. This was the moment I met Ronald.

On the screen I have a shocked look on my face. I said, "Um...

yeah..." got up, stuck my hand through the bars and shook the empty air. "I'm Nik."

My mind turned to mush as he showed me clip after clip. Me having conversations with the thin air. Me sitting in my bunk appearing to turn pages of a book that isn't there. Me sitting on my blanket in the middle of a cell on that scratchy wool blanket pantomiming the reading of a book before taking a heavy breath and flexing my shoulders.

I can't think. How could this be possible? I had never read any Jack Reacher novels, yet I could tell you the plots of the many that Ronald had brought me. I could describe to you exactly what Ronald's face looked like, the melodic timber of his voice, the slightly yellowish color of his teeth.

"But... I..." I said, my voice thick and pleading, so much so that I couldn't stand it.

My interrogator took a deep breath and let out a sigh. "It is concerning, isn't it?"

I looked at him. There was a sparkle in his eye. The bastard was enjoying this.

"Maybe we should go back to this Byte woman," he intoned, just like I was in the interrogation room. "Surely there is something else you can tell me about her."

I surged against my restraints, I wanted to hurt him. I wanted to punch him, to throw him across the room, to beat him until the tone of his voice showed some emotion. But I couldn't. I was strapped to the bed and could barely move at all. An inelegant grunt escaped me.

"Or we could talk about the conversation you had with Toxicwasteman after the breach of the Hoover Dam," he said calmly.

He hadn't told me that Ronald wasn't real or shown me that footage for my own benefit. He had done it to further unbalance me, to break me, to get me to spill the secrets he knew I was keeping.

He was cruel. And right then and there, I would have preferred

Tom Tyree over him. I would have rather been his prisoner. Tom's motives and methods were at least clear. This man was something I didn't understand and something I didn't want to understand.

My mind slipped back to when I was in the cell. When Evan Saunders actually talked to me. When I was convinced that I had found a way to turn into Neutrinoman without a nuclear reactor. When I had tried and blacked out and ended up here.

I turned away from my interrogator and took a deep breath, letting my eyes half close and staring up at the ceiling of the infirmary. He kept talking but his voice was just like the tornado of thoughts running through my head. I let them go and focused on my breath. I wanted to find that place again and hoped that now that I was a bit healthier, I could manage the transformation. That I could turn into Neutrinoman. That I could escape this prison and this man I had come to hate so much.

EMPATHY. IT'S AN IMPORTANT SKILL TO HAVE. ALSO, realizing that everyone is the hero of their own story. Tom Tyree, my interrogator when I was in prison, and whoever had their finger on the trigger of Project Vulcan. They had reasons to do what they were doing.

Maybe it was because I had just meditated, but after Licia charged me and we walked back to the excavation site, I tried to imagine the person that had conceived of and controlled Project Vulcan.

They must believe that we could easily become more of a threat than anything that we might be called to defend against. And I could see that. If Licia and I decided to go all Bonnie and Clyde, it would be bad.

They must believe that the alien threat is done, despite how things turned out.

They must be afraid of what we could do to usurp the status quo.

Having empathy doesn't mean you don't defend yourself. As

we walked, her electric hand in my neutrino hand, our yellow and blue-white glow lighting up the desert, I understood their motivation. I was hoping whoever was watching would understand mine.

"What should I do?" Licia asked. We were on the edge of the pit staring down. Now that it was time, we both were hesitating.

I looked at her scintillating face, at the worry there. "Stay alive," I said. She gave me a wan smile and nodded. I looked back to the home we had built with our own two hands. "We might lose everything, you know."

"The only thing I need is you," she said. It was sappy and romantic and filled my heart with joy. I kissed her, our bodies doing their energy exchange, taking our passion and our love and our worry and multiplying it. We took our time with that kiss, not knowing, yet again, if there would be another. When it was done, I jumped into the pit.

I took a deep breath and calmed myself. I don't have to breathe in the normal sense as Neutrinoman. I don't need the oxygen. But it helps even in my q-morph form to calm me. It took a few minutes but the sight came back, only more powerfully. I could see the purple ball of energy down and over. I could see a tiny line of blue leading to it—some kind of power or communication running to the east.

I went to the north edge of our pit, ramped up my reaction, and started melting the earth around me. I took my time. I knew they knew what I was doing. This was more about seeing if they had the will to pull the trigger. If preventing us from discovering it was more important than our lives.

Still, it was only fifty feet. It didn't take long. I melted a roughly cylindrical tunnel straight down and then I broke into a cavern. It was small, maybe ten feet in diameter, and there in the middle of it was an odd-looking shape, basically rectangular, but with a few non-right angles all covered in gleaming stainless steel. It was about the size of a VW Bug. Project Vulcan.

The cave didn't look natural. It had a uniform shape that made it look like it was mechanically excavated. There were metal supports lining the ceiling and unlit bare lightbulbs attached to the supports.

And beyond the cave, which was lit by the flickering yellow of my neutrino reaction was a tunnel, and I could faintly hear voices.

22 / OUR LITTLE SECRET

THE DRONE OF MY INTERROGATOR WENT ON, THE ASSAULT OF my own doubts and fears continued, time slowly slipped past as my half-slitted eyes gazed at the fluorescent light above, my body relaxed on the infirmary table, my ankles and wrists strapped securely.

Meditation is hard work. Really hard. It may not sound like it or look like it, but it is. In many ways I find it similar to running. Getting started on it is difficult, painful, and taxing, but once you get over the hump it remains hard, but it is rewarding. The meditator's high, if you will.

Meditating when some sick bastard is trying to break you, keeps reminding you that the man you've been interacting with for the last six months wasn't real, is all too happy to keep proving it to you, wants nothing more than to break your spirit, is beyond difficult.

But the level of difficulty was irrelevant, though. I had to do it. I had to calm myself and reach deep inside and find that trigger, turn myself into Neutrinoman.

While he continued to ask me about Byte and Tom Tyree and

the base they took me to, and the other members of LoVE I had met, I kept meditating, focusing on my breath, on that sensation as air passed in and out of my nose. While I worried that he would go nuts and kill me, that I would never see Licia again, or that if I did, she would either have not waited for me or not want me anymore. I kept letting those thoughts go and focused on my breath. While I worried about the alien threat to our planet and how powerless I was to do anything about it, I kept breathing deeply and evenly.

Our view of how our minds should work (neat, clean, and orderly) and how they really work (a chaotic swirl of everything from hope to despair several times a second) had become clear to me. That is the one thing I gained from Ronald (real or not) and my time in prison and my time reading *A Gradual Awakening* (real or not).

The human mind is a messy thing that by some miracle ends up working.

As I kept letting go and kept breathing, my body relaxed. I found myself not resisting my interrogator but becoming more open. So open that his words just passed right through, becoming insubstantial ghosts.

I felt the air flowing through my nose as it made its way into my lungs. I felt my belly expand with each inhale and grow relaxed with each exhale. I noticed the smooth texture of the sheet below me and the slight breeze from the room's ventilation.

Slowly I noticed a blue nimbus around the fluorescent lights, then I could see a pulsing in the ceiling of the wire that brought power to the light. I didn't dwell on it, I went deeper.

I heard the guard outside the infirmary door shifting his position, taking a deep breath, and sighing. My hearing became even better than normal.

I could feel the radiation emanating from the fixture. Visible light and electromagnetic radiation. Electromagnetic radiation coming from the man next to me.

I opened up to it. I breathed it in. I am Neutrinoman. I am the power of the split atom itself. Radiation is everywhere. It is enough to trigger my transformation.

And there it was. That switch. I could turn right then and there. I knew it. I finally had it.

"What did Tom Tyree tell you on the way to Yellowstone?" he asked. "We should go back there to the first time you were alone with him. Maybe that is where it all started."

His words didn't mean much to me and they were still smooth and steady, but in my state of heightened awareness I could hear the tension below the surface, I could smell his fearful sweat. He was about to fail. He was desperate.

It wasn't a thought, not really, it was more of a sense of empathy for my captor and a knowing that if I turned with him this close, I would hurt him, maybe kill him. A few minutes ago, that would have been fine with me, but now that I had heard and smelled his fear, I hesitated. His failure would have personal ramifications. Did he really deserve to die?

I was aware he had moved away from the bed, but it wasn't important. I was following my breath, letting go of my thoughts, trying to stay deep enough to flip that switch. So when I felt the prick at my arm, I was surprised.

"Shhh," he said, a wicked smile on his face. "Chemical induce-ments were forbidden—we mustn't risk real damage to our mighty superhero. But who could have imagined you'd fracture like this with your invisible friend and all? We don't have much time left, so what can it hurt? We'll let this be our little secret."

The syringe had a clear liquid in it and he quickly injected it. I felt a slithering cold invade my artery as my blood started mixing with the clear substance. What was it? His green eyes were alight. His mouth forming a childlike smile.

I knew I didn't have much time. I reached for that switch that would turn me into Neutrinoman. I flipped the switch. I triggered the transformation.

23 / TRANSFORMATION

I AM A QUANTUM METAMORPH. I CHANGE AT A QUANTUM level, every cell in my body becomes this different thing. My basic structure is the same: two arms, two legs, two eyes, a lung cavity. But the function becomes different. I become a nuclear reaction, not a biochemical one.

When I am strong, fully powered, the transformation can be fast, like a fire through a parched forest. And when I am weak the transformation can be very slow, starting at a single point and spreading a millimeter at a time like a slow water leak on a bathroom floor.

In that underground prison with my interrogator desperate and injecting me with a clear substance, my point of focus was on that injection, that slithering sensation of cold. That is where the transformation started. The inside of my right elbow.

I was in a strange state. Half scared, half meditative. The threat seemed real and distant at the same time.

My nose was still biological, so I smelled the sharp scent of my neutrino-self combined with the smokey smell of the sheet below my arm starting to smolder.

My interrogator's eyes widened, and he stepped back. "No..." he muttered, some emotion finally entering his voice.

I kept breathing, kept willing myself to transform. First the inside of my elbow, then the yellow swirl of my neutrino form traveled down my arm to my wrist, the restraints there starting to smolder.

It was going so slowly. I needed to be out of here, I needed to be free.

Curiosity bloomed on his face, his green eyes going to my changed arm, his back against the infirmary's counter. "Did I do that?"

I almost laughed. He thought the injection had changed me, not my will. With the transformation starting there, I could see how he got that idea. I didn't correct him. I kept focusing on my breath, focusing on my transformation. My transformed right hand broke free of the restraint, smoke now visible in the air. I ripped off my other restraints and stood as my body continued its slow transformation, my grey prison jumpsuit starting to smolder.

"I'm leaving now," I said. I was still transforming, my right arm and leg now a pulsing yellow, the rest of me still flesh, my clothes burning off me. It was a strange feeling, this slow-motion transformation.

"I don't think so," he said with a grin.

A blaring alarm went off as I heard the slap of boots on the floor outside the room. At the same time the sprinklers above us opened up and water started raining down on us.

Two more breaths and the transformation was finally complete. I no longer felt the water that fell on me only to sizzle away as steam.

"Get out of my way. I don't want to hurt you," I said.

"We both know that's not true." He was standing in front of the door, daring me to go through him, daring me to hurt him.

While I was fully transformed, my reaction was low and tenuous. I didn't feel my normal Neutrinoman self.

I shrugged, turned to the nearest wall and plunged my hand into it and started cutting through.

I didn't have much of a plan besides escape.

My interrogator opened the door and let the guards in. It was the usual three. Evan Saunders with a rifle this time, the ubiquitous M4 carbine the military loves, and the two other guards with alien energy weapons.

"Stand down," Saunders yelled at me over the fire alarm, the water soaking through his black clothing.

I turned to them. "I don't want to hurt anyone. Just let me go."

"Can't do that," Evan said. He was back to being a soldier with orders. What he would do wasn't going to change by me giving a speech.

"Okay," I said, stepping away from the small hole I had made in the wall. I could see that there was a supply room on the other side. "But you'll have to do something for me."

"Stand down," Evan said. "Now!"

I ignored him and backed up to the bed I had been strapped down to. "All I want is to talk to Colonel Williams. If you can guarantee a face-to-face with him, I will cooperate."

Evan glanced at the other two soldiers. My interrogator was gone, he had slipped out of the room after the soldiers came in. They all looked scared. "Fire," Evan shouted and I ran for the hole I had created.

"WHAT SHOULD WE DO?" LIGHTNINGIRL ASKED, LOOKING AT the bomb that sat below our high desert home. There wasn't much to see, just a large, roughly rectangular shape covered in stainless-steel plates sitting in a rough-hewn cavern. No "Project Vulcan" on the side. No urgent red countdown lights. No switches or controls. I had flown up and brought her back down so we could investigate together.

"This thing has power running through it and leading to it," I said and then pointed to the thick black cable. "But it's not an active power." My sight, my EMV or Electromagnetic Vision, was still working. "There is an element to it that reminds me of the alien energy weapons, but I think there is more."

"Maybe you should open it up," she said.

I shook my head. "I heard voices before I came to get you. I say we leave this for now and find out what else is here."

She eyed the bomb again suspiciously and nodded. I took her hand, enjoying our energy exchange, and we slowly walked down the tunnel. I heard the faint voices again. They were low and urgent.

The tunnel was long, several hundred yards, and towards its end we could see light up ahead and I heard other sounds to go with the voices. The clacking of keyboards. Footfalls. The whisper of ventilation.

The tunnel stopped at an oversized metal door. I dampened down my reaction in my right hand and tried it. It was locked. The voices had stopped.

"What now?" I asked.

Licia shrugged and knocked on the door, the metallic clang echoing down the long tunnel behind us.

"I know you're there," I shouted. "I'd really rather not blast the door down."

There were furtive whispers, the sounds of boots, a scrape and a click as the door was unlocked, and then a groan as the big door was swung back.

When I saw who waited for us, my jaw dropped. It was Agent Peters, the Homeland Security agent that oversaw us. The bland, bald man that Licia charmed and I avoided as much as possible. The thorn in our side that insisted we fill out the proper paperwork and follow all the rules. I thought he was just a bureaucrat who got the crappy job of looking after us.

Licia didn't miss a beat, though. "I expect explanations, and I expect them now."

The room behind Peters looked like your average office building. Fluorescent lighting, linoleum on the floor, desks lining the walls with large monitors, it only lacked windows. The mundanity of it was very incongruent.

Peters looked back to the other three people in the room and then back at us. They were all dressed like him in black suits as the Homeland people always were. "Perhaps I should meet you back at your place," he said, his voice wavering.

"I don't know," I said to Licia. "I'd like a tour. Wouldn't you like a tour?"

"Yes, dear," she said with an electrical smile. "I'd like a tour too." She looked back to Peters. "Perhaps you can get us some robes or something so we don't do any damage while you show us around."

He didn't speak, his jaw silently moving. This was obviously not a contingency they planned for. "Alison," he said to a young, dark-haired woman I had seen a few times. "See what you can find our guests." She got up quickly and left through another door.

"Maybe we should all go wait by the bomb," I offered. "Or, maybe you should start telling us what is going on. Right now."

He went pale, which was quite satisfying, but didn't move.

"Come on, John," Licia said. "I think you owe us some sort of explanation."

His eyes were twitching back and forth between us. We were still in our q-morph forms, so maybe he was worried about radiation, maybe something else was going on.

A paranoid thought crept into my mind. What if he was stalling us until the bomb goes off. Maybe they were willing to sacrifice themselves too.

I thought back to the bomb. It had some of the latent energy of an alien energy weapon—that's how I saw it. Williams had characterized it more of an explosive device. It clicked in my mind. It was a huge alien energy weapon combined with a massive explosion. It would strip us of our powers so that the explosion would then kill us.

I squeezed Lightningirl's hand. "We're leaving now," I said to her and then turned to Peters. "Get your people out of here. I don't want anyone to get hurt."

"What? You can't..." Peters stammered.

"What is it?" Licia asked.

"Now!" I shouted at Peters. "We're coming in."

Peters's eyes kept ping-ponging between Licia and me. He

backed up a step but didn't go farther. The other two suits in the room were staring at us.

"Trust me, honey," I said. Her lips pursed, but she nodded. "Now get these people moving!"

She extended her right hand, tiny bolts of electricity stabbing out from her fingers to Peters and the other two agents. "You heard the man," she said. "We're leaving. Now! Lead the way."

With yelps of pain, the three of them scurried out of the room.

I closed the large metal door behind me and noticed that the entire back wall of this room was made of metal. It wouldn't be enough to shield from the blast, not completely. But it would be helpful if there was radiation involved. If the bomb had a nuclear component... well, a very small nuclear component.

Licia and the rest had left the room. I paused, looking at the flat screens. One had paused aerial footage of Licia and I digging the root cellar. Another showed the transcript of a recent conversation we had had. Yet another showed the exact route of a walk we had taken two days ago.

Anger welled up in me in this underground facility. It reminded me of the prison I had been "detained" in so many years ago. It brought back the sense of claustrophobia. I could almost hear the voice of my interrogator asking me about Tom Tyree and Byte.

With a cry, I shot each of the flat screens with a neutrino bolt, and then shot everything in sight. Sparks flew and a small fire started on one of the desks. I kept blasting, shouting words that I don't remember. When Lightningirl came for me, the room was dark except for the yellow glow of my reaction, the flickering of the fire, and the blue-white light her lightning form cast.

"Honey," she shouted. "We need to go!"

I could feel the tingle of her electrical touch, but I was far away. The remnants of fluorescent lights dangled from the ceiling. I blasted them into bits.

"Nik!" she shouted, pulling me towards the door and out of the room.

I would not be a prisoner, even in our lovely high desert home. I could not be a prisoner. Not anymore.

The thick bolt of lightning she struck me with got my attention. I looked back at her, her electrical hair haloed around her beautiful but worried face. She was tapping into the electrical supply of this facility, which must be considerable.

I took a deep breath. The hall behind her, again, looked like any other office building with linoleum and horrible fluorescent lighting that was flickering as Lightningirl drew power. It had a haze of smoke from the fires I had started, but was otherwise empty.

A small lightning bolt leapt out of the wall to her left hand. The power line must have been just below the surface. The wall was blackening and was now on fire too.

Another breath and I nodded.

"I want to bring this place down," I shouted so she could hear me above the crackle of the lightning. "Are they all out?"

She nodded, the worried look not leaving her face.

"Keep feeding me power." I turned my back to her and started blasting the ceiling as we walked backwards down the hallway. This was unacceptable. This I could not leave.

Rock fell as the hallway we had just left collapsed, dust engulfing us.

I had felt change was coming, but this was unlike anything I had imagined.

IN THE INFIRMARY OF THE Q-MORPH PRISON, THIS WAS NO longer me figuring out something crucial about my powers. This was now life and death. All three of them fired at once. Two alien energy weapons and one semiautomatic rifle.

As I hit the wall it slowed me down and two of the purple energy balls hit me. One in my right leg, one square in the back. I could feel my meager reaction dimming, my right leg going numb. Several bullets passed through me too, but this wasn't a problem. Yet.

Once the energy weapons turned me back to flesh, the bullets would matter.

Evan Saunders who likes soccer not football, whose girl didn't wait for him while he was in Iraq, was trying to kill me. This was war now. Could I take his life to preserve my own? A man who was just following orders?

And is that even an excuse? "Just following orders" has been used throughout the ages to justify a myriad of sins.

I was in a jumble in the supply room floor lying on top of metal shelves I had knocked over on my way through, rolls of toilet paper on top of me catching on fire. I shot several neutrino bolts through the hole in the wall up into the ceiling of the infirmary. At the same time purple energy balls came flying through the hole well above me.

The smoke was starting to get thick and the sprinklers went off in this room too. I rolled off the shelf, and staying low, made it to the door. My right leg was really slowing me down. While I blindly shot neutrino bolts through the hole, I looked at my leg. It was a duller yellow, the nuclear reaction there having slowed.

I had transformed without the tiniest bit of direct radiation, surely I could deal with this.

But there wasn't time. One of the soldiers peeked through the hole in the wall and fired, the coruscating purple energy ball flying right above my head. I fired neutrino bolts at him and he disappeared.

I needed a plan. I needed a way out. I needed a serious source of energy.

I yanked the door open, the metal melting under my brief touch, and hobbled out into the hallway.

They were ready for me. I didn't stand a chance.

FALL 2005, LOCATION UNKNOWN

Down in that prison made for q-morphs, far below the ground, two guards stood at each end of the hallway I had just hobbled out into, both of them pointing alien energy weapons at me. Big beefy boys dressed in black. Neither of them familiar to me.

They didn't wait. They didn't ask questions. They fired.

I went down, lying flat on the wet floor, steam rising up as my reaction touched the water from the sprinklers.

I felt the energy balls fly above me. It was a sensation very similar to the hairs on the back of your neck rising up. Except I had no hair, I was completely neutrino. I could feel their energy. I could feel my own energy wanting to go to it. Opposites attract. Those energy balls were the opposite of my neutronic energy somehow. That's why they affected me the way they did. I thought furiously about it. They were energy, surely there was a way for me to tap it, instead of its energy canceling out my own.

I didn't have long to think about it. Right after the energy balls passed above me, I heard high-pitched squeals coming from either end of the hallway and then there was an explosion.

The floor beneath me shook and I felt blast waves crash into me from either direction. I focused on maintaining my neutrino form, on remaining calm, remaining alive.

If I had been biological, I would have been dead. From the shockwave, from the heat.

Those energy balls that the alien weapons shoot don't always act the same. Well... they always tap my powers, but sometimes they explode on contact, like the first time I saw them in Yellowstone. I've also seen them do no harm whatsoever to physical objects. I also knew that they could fire orange energy balls that tapped Lightningirl's powers.

So when I heard the explosion, I was baffled at first. The coruscating purple color had been a bit pale, the variety that didn't do physical damage, so why would they explode?

From my prone position, I looked down the hallway. There wasn't much left of the guards and the floor. The walls and ceiling had been carved out in an eerily perfect, spherical shape, digging into the rock beyond the walls. I turned in the other direction and there was a spherical blast there too. I saw Evan and his two men coming out of the infirmary, shaking their heads, their eyes wide as they saw the guard's blast areas and what little was left of him. A hand, a foot with clean cuts, and no blood like they had been carefully cut off a department store dummy.

"What... What the hell?" Evan stammered.

"I didn't do it," I shouted. "They both shot those weapons at the same time... and... and..."

Evan wiped the falling water from his face and stared. This wasn't normal. He was trying to figure out what to do.

I was too. I decided to run.

The base near Casita de Soledad wasn't large. That first room was the control room, and besides that it had a small kitchen, a dormitory, and some bathrooms and showers. And then a long hallway leading to a large garage.

I blasted all of it. Licia tried to stop me several times, but I couldn't do it. It was too much like that prison. I was too infuriated by what I had seen on those monitors.

We q-morphs had given all we could in our battle against the aliens, many of us our lives. We had saved the planet time and time again. It hadn't been perfect, and it hadn't been pretty, but this is how they rewarded us? Put us on our q-morph reservations and monitored our every move? Planted a bomb under us to take us out if we become a threat?

I had been so naïve to not expect that. I was mad at myself, not just them.

The garage was hidden in a cliff next to that poor excuse for a road that led to Casita de Soledad. We were less than a mile, as the raven flies, from our house, in a shallow canyon that Licia and I never roamed to, our wanderings keeping us closer to home and on more friendly terrain. I had always thought the agents had to drive a long way to get to us. But no. They had been in the neighborhood the whole time.

The agents were out of the garage and in their big black SUVs when we got there.

"Leave," I said to Peters who was standing in front of the first one. "I don't know what the radius of that bomb is, but I don't expect you want to be here when I deal with it."

"Stop now," Peters said, his voice calm, his spine erect. "The further you go, the worse this will be."

I walked up to him, banking my reaction way down. "I am going to give you some time to clear out. My wife is fond of you. But let me tell you this right now, this had best be the last time I see you."

His brow furrowed and his grey eyes pinched. "They are not going to like this," he said.

"Then have them come talk directly to me," I said. "Now go. I'll give you thirty minutes."

Peters's shoulders fell, and he got into the passenger's side seat of the SUV. The vehicles made their slow way down the road. I stood silently until they were out of sight.

When I turned back, I had the goddess of electricity staring at me, her stance wide, her hands on her hips. "You had best explain yourself," Lightningirl said.

28 / LARRY WHO RAISES FLOWERS

As I RAN DOWN THE HALLWAY OF MY PRISON, MY BODY THE yellow motes of q-morph form, a purple energy ball clipped my left shoulder as I came to the pit that one of the explosions had created, I went tumbling in. It was a sphere about twelve feet in diameter, cutting deeply into the bedrock this facility was carved out of. I thought back to the guards' positions when I had come out into the hallway. They had been on either side of me in that long hallway.

Both guards had shot their energy weapons at me at pretty much the same time. I had ducked. The energy balls had gone over me and impacted the opposite guard.

That whining noise I had heard had been those huge power packs they wore on their backs. They had exploded and vaporized the guards and the hallway.

Shoot an alien energy weapon with an alien energy weapon and... boom.

There were bits of smoldering cloth and other things at the bottom of the pit that I didn't want to try to identify. I felt for the guards. I hated that they were dead, but this was not my doing.

As bullets and energy balls passed above me, I looked at the sides and top of the sphere. It was smooth like the blast had vaporized the rock, water dripping on me from above from the mostly sealed end of a water pipe. I was hoping for an escape route, but there was rock all around. I remembered the long elevator ride we had taken when they had brought me here. We were deep below the earth and I certainly didn't have enough power to tunnel my way out.

Casting about for a plan, I decided to fire neutrino bolts into the ceiling down the hallway, to create a barrier and buy some time.

I was about to proceed when I noticed that the firing had stopped. It was still noisy, water dripping on me and hissing up into steam.

"Nik, I have ordered my men to stop firing," my interrogator said, his voice smooth and confident. "I would like to talk before there is more loss of life."

"Tell me your name first," I shouted. "Your real name." It may seem like an odd request, but I needed some sliver of humanity from this man that had imprisoned me, isolated me, starved me, tried to drug me into talking.

There was a pause. I thought back to the interrogation room when I surmised that those pauses were him talking to his superiors, but when I had been in the infirmary, he had told me he was in charge. Maybe he just thought before he spoke.

The sprinklers suddenly shut off and the silence seemed vast, just the drip-drip of water.

"My name is Larry," he said.

"Tell me something about yourself, Larry." I said. The hallway was full of steam still and I couldn't see him.

"I don't see how that is—" he began.

"You said you wanted to talk," I said. "So let's have a conversation."

Another pause. "I like flowers," he said, a reluctance in his smooth voice as if talking about himself was painful. "I like to raise flowers."

I tried to imagine Larry with his green eyes and sharp cheekbones fussing over petunias or maybe orchids. The image was congruent, and I decided he was telling the truth.

"Thank you, Larry. So what is it you want to talk about?"

"I told you earlier you were going to be released." His voice was back to being as smooth as ever. "I wasn't lying. There is no need for this."

When he had injected me, it had been a desperation move. He wanted to get my secrets out of me before I left. Perhaps preserving his prison and his life had taken precedence over that need.

"What do you propose?" I asked.

"That you revert your form," he said. "That I walk you out of here right now."

"No," I said. "I don't trust you, Larry. You just tried to drug the truth out of me not ten minutes ago."

"And for that I am sorry," he said, the faintest trace of emotion in his voice. "I lost my way and won't try anything again."

I thought about it lying on the earth in the bottom of that sphere, my reaction low and tenuous. The water was gone, all having turned to steam.

"I want Saunders," I said. "I want to hear you give him orders to escort me out immediately, to not attempt me harm. And I don't want to see your face anywhere. Do you understand?"

Another pause. "Yes," Larry said. "I accept your terms."

That made me nervous. It was too easy.

I listened carefully as he issued orders to Evan and my other two regular guards. I didn't hear anything that bothered me, that might let them turn on me. And that really bothered me.

SUMMER 2025, CASITA DE SOLEDAD, CENTRAL ARIZONA

OUR HOME SEEMED DIFFERENT AFTER WE WALKED BACK HAND in hand, still in our quantum forms. It had a silence that made it feel like it had been abandoned for a long time. Our little adobe house, the two green houses, my tool shed, and the pit for the root cellar with its tunnel down to the bomb.

We stood there staring at that tunnel.

"Are you sure?" Lightningirl asked.

We had talked there in front of the base for a long time. I honestly expected them to trigger the bomb once their people were out of its radius. But they didn't. It had been an hour. It had been long enough for them to get clear.

I nodded. "We can't live this way, can we?" After I had explained how like the prison this was, she had agreed with my plan. I just wanted to hear her say again.

"No," she said, her jaw set. "We cannot."

"There will be consequences," I said.

"These are the consequences they brought on by doing this to us." The anger in her voice was palpable. I had told her what I saw on those screens, to what degree they had been monitoring us. Williams had told us as much, but seeing it made it that much worse, that much more real.

I nodded, walked over to our beautiful house that we built with our own two hands. I let go of my q-morph form before entering. I couldn't damage it, not directly, not intentionally. Licia followed, grabbing my hand after we entered. I felt eerily calm, and the sight, somehow, was still with me.

I quickly found the three cameras in our living room. I didn't have any idea if the feeds went beyond the destroyed base, but their presence was unacceptable. I pointed them out to Licia, she transformed just her right hand and she fried them, tiny lightning bolts jabbing from her finger to the cameras.

It didn't take long. We went through each room of the house and she destroyed any hidden electronics.

I felt the fool. I shouldn't have trusted them. I should have looked for them earlier.

And then finally, once we knew we were truly alone, I pulled the cookie tin from under our bed. It was a faded red with a picture of Santa Claus on it. I opened it up and pulled out the black metal case inside of it.

"One of Tom's many gifts," I said to Licia.

She smiled, a strained gesture, but didn't speak.

The black case was heavy and it clanged on our tile floor when I set it down. I opened it slowly, reverently. The walls of the case were thick, made of lead, and the inside compartment was small. Sitting there was a little black bag.

I pulled it out and poured the contents onto my hand. Little grey rocks, they didn't look like anything, but I could feel the energy in them, the power waiting to be unlocked.

They were from that LoVE base that I had visited and where Tom had tried to recruit me before I met the alien Sarah. These little rocks were uranium ore.

I stood and walked out of the house over to the pit.

"How much are you going to use," Licia asked.

We stood there naked under the summer sun. I knew they were watching now. They had cameras external to our house, but I didn't want to take the time to go find them and they certainly had drones, and what could I do about them?

Down through the dirt I could see the coiled purple ball of energy that was the bomb.

"All of it," I said as I turned into Neutrinoman. The uranium ore absorbing into my q-morph form.

This wasn't pure uranium, like what I had fallen in in the bottom of the pit in Yellowstone when we first encountered the aliens. But it was a significant charge. I hadn't felt this powerful in years. Not since I had had access to a nuclear reactor.

Licia changed to Lightningirl and I took her into my arms and flew straight up. Our property rapidly receded until we were about a thousand feet up. Everything looked small, like they were just toys, some kind of desert diorama made for a school project.

"Are you sure?" I asked her again. Sure that she was okay with me doing this. Sure that she wouldn't leave and get herself out of danger's way before I tried it. After Peters had left and I had explained myself, we had argued over this.

"I am still sure," she said. "We stand together, or we..." she trailed off, not finishing the thought.

"I love you," I said.

"I love you, too," she said.

I thrusted hard for several seconds then switched from thrusting to firing neutrino bolts. I rained hell down upon the pit we had dug, down the tunnel I had melted, all the way to that bomb.

It was time to be free.

FALL 2005, GROOM LAKE, NEVADA

THE SUN WAS BRIGHT, ITS RAYS HARSH ON MY EYES THAT HAD been underground and deprived of it for so long. But my skin, it reveled at the exposure of the UV radiation. I felt like a tourist coming out onto a Hawaiian beach after a long Midwest winter. The warm breeze felt like heaven compared to the stale recycled air down there.

Except I wasn't a tourist and this wasn't a vacation.

Evan Saunders and the other two guards had escorted me out of the prison. They had handguns and rifles, but no more energy weapons. After seeing what happened to the other guards, I couldn't imagine they wanted those energy packs on their backs.

I hadn't seen my interrogator, Larry, since we made our deal and the guards and I hadn't talked much on the long walk through the corridors or on the ride up the elevator. They had brought me another dull grey prison jumpsuit and I had put it on. I didn't have shoes, so I could feel every pebble under my feet.

The land was dry and flat in front of us with brown craggy hills poking out here and there. There was a large and very flat expanse of white not far in front of us, and past that an airfield and some squat buildings. We were just north of Groom Lake in Area 51.

I felt my face flush with anger. All that time Licia and I were training here, they had been building a prison for us.

"They're sending a jeep," Evan said, his chin poking out towards the military base. "It'll be a little bit. They weren't expecting us so soon."

Behind us was a small cinder block building with a single metal door and no windows. Innocuous. You wouldn't think it was anything. But I knew better.

I swayed and Evan grabbed my elbow, keeping me from toppling over. I was weak and dehydrated. Turning into Neutrinoman with no charge was, I now knew, possible, but it came with a price.

"Do you need to sit, sir?" he asked.

It seemed funny him calling me "sir."

I shook my head. I wanted to stay on my feet. "So who is your favorite soccer team?" I asked.

He smiled briefly before his eyes went back to the white expanse, searching for our ride. "I root for the US, of course," he said. "But I love the Brazilian national team. Such skill. Such passion."

"I've never watched much soccer," I began, so glad to just be chatting. "It seems a little tame compared to—"

"Incoming!" shouted one of the other guards. The one with brown hair that always had the cuffs on the pole when they came and got me for interrogation.

What was he talking about? Incoming? Did he mean a missile or something? My brain was sluggish and soon I was knocked over and felt a heavy body on top of me before I heard and felt an explosion behind me. Remnants of the brick building rained down on us. Evan grunted as he took the bulk of the impact.

Who would be attacking us here? We were on a military base, for God's sake. Was this part of my interrogator's plan?

I was still dazed as automatic gunfire rang out and I felt the spray of dirt on my face from bullets hitting the ground near me. Evan dragged me behind the rubble of the building. The attack was coming from the north, from the craggy rock that rose out of the desert on the far side of Groom Lake.

One of the guards was talking, calling for help. The other guard was firing his rifle, an M4 carbine, popping up from the rubble and shooting up into the hills, the shots barking out in short bursts.

Evan was talking to me, but I was still dazed and didn't understand him.

The guard with the gun popped up again but then he fell back in a jumbled heap, blood at this temple.

Evan was shaking me then, and his words finally reached me. "...change. You must change into Neutrinoman. You must do it now. You must survive."

The bright blue sky framed Evan's head and complemented his green eyes. He looked serious and scared. He looked desperate. He had been my guard, what did he care if I survived?

He slapped me, hard. "Goddamnit, snap out of it. The world needs you."

I nodded and took a deep breath. "I need a moment."

"I'll give you what I can," he said.

The remaining two guards started firing up at the hill. I didn't know how many assailants there were, but it seemed like a lot. I heard the faint roar of a helicopter in the distance, but it was going to be too late. I needed to change now.

But I couldn't find that switch. I was too weak. I was slumped in the sun and didn't know what to do.

Then I remembered Ronald, with his elegant demeanor and his long fingers. The meditation book. That is how I did it before.

I half closed my eyes and gazed up at the sun. Taking in every bit of radiation I could. I turned away from my tornado of fears and doubts and started focusing on my breath. Feeling the passage of air through my nose, feeling my belly rise and fall. I was aware of my other guard, the one that always had the energy weapon, going down. I let it go. I went back to my breath. I dove as deep and fast as I could.

"Now or never," Evan hissed. "I'm out of ammo."

The gunfire stopped and the silence hastened my descent into my mind. Time passed, I don't know how much, but I heard a helicopter getting closer, I heard the crunch of boots on the desert sand.

"Stand aside, son," a deep voice said. "I don't want you."

I was not looking at him, our attacker. I was vaguely surprised it was just one person, but I let that go and focused on my breath. I wasn't really looking at him, but I could tell that he was tall and strong, his presence looming over my emaciated form. Evan was there standing between the two of us.

Evan lunged at him and was thrown aside. I let it go, following my breath, looking for the trigger. I let the thought of looking for the trigger go and went back to my breath.

I knew I wasn't going to make it but let go of that thought too. The figure was pointing a gun at me, but still I wasn't looking at him. I was gazing up at the sun, my body still drinking in all the radiation that I could.

"Nothing personal," he said.

Things slowed down. I heard my heart beating in my ears. My mouth sour and dry. I felt the heat of the sun warming and energizing me. I heard the shuffle of feet and the cocking of a gun's hammer.

I was close. So close. But not there yet. I needed more time.

I let it all go and focused on my breath.

The hammer fell. The gun fired.

31 / VULCAN

VULCAN IS THE ANCIENT ROMAN GOD OF FIRE. HE WAS associated with both the destructive and fertilizing aspects of fire. Fire, it can destroy, but it also can create.

Williams had called the bomb, "Project Vulcan." Maybe the Vulcan referred to me—I was the most fiery of the q-morphs. Maybe it referred to the fire the bomb would unleash. Maybe the name was chosen by someone who was into *Star Trek*. It didn't matter.

The first neutrino bolts didn't do much but extend the pit we had dug and collapse the tunnel I had melted. It didn't matter. I was well powered. I started a rhythm. Thrust up until we had good upward momentum and then shoot neutrino bolts out of my hands and feet.

Licia clung to the front of me fiercely. The girl hates to fly and this was the worst kind. We were flying then falling then flying again.

I maintained my altitude above one thousand feet. I had no

idea what the blast radius was. That was as high as I thought I could go and still hit the target.

I missed several times and took out our new greenhouse. Lightningirl didn't say a word, her strangling grip on my neck tightening only slightly.

I could still see the ball of restrained purple energy below the earth. I just kept at it. Flying, firing, flying, firing.

And then it happened.

The little purple energy ball began to expand rapidly, like a spring let loose from its containment. I stopped firing and flew up as fast as I could.

But it wasn't fast enough. Not nearly enough.

32 / AN UNACCEPTABLE SACRIFICE

IT's NOT LIKE DECIDING TO SCRATCH YOUR NOSE, TURNING into Neutrinoman, that is. It's an act of will, but a bit of a tricky one. It's more like sneezing. When the time is right, when the forces within you need it, sneezing is easy. When your nose is clear it's almost impossible to sneeze for real. I mean you can do an awkward ahh-choo, but that is no real sneeze.

Willing myself to turn into Neutrinoman is kind of like that. Easy and natural when I'm fully powered. Awkward and difficult when I am not.

And lying there in Area 51 not far from Groom Lake, my half-closed gaze on the sun, my body already spent from my time in prison and my recent unpowered change to Neutrinoman, it was more than awkward. It was nearly impossible.

When our attacker's gun fired, the sharp sound of it just about burst my eardrum and the sand of the desert splattered my face. He missed on purpose. The thought was a bright spark in my mind, but I let it go and breathed. Almost there.

"I expected more out of you," the attacker said. He sounded

sad, regretful. "Fight me, at least, will you? What the hell happened to you down there?"

He was talking like he knew me. That thought lingered briefly before I let it go too. There was one way out of this. I had to go deeper.

"Oh well," he said. It was time, but I wasn't quite there. Any attempt at change would still be like a fake sneeze, not a real one.

There was a grunt, the sharp retort of a gun firing echoing out over the land, and the sound of bodies falling to the ground.

Evan Saunders, who likes soccer, who had a girl once, had tackled our attacker, had saved my life.

I'm so close. I can feel the switch, just out of reach. I let the thought go and breathed.

They struggled and grunted on the desert floor. I saw bits of it in my peripheral vision, the sun still dominating my field of vision. One of them let out a feral scream. It was like an animal that wanted blood, that would kill to survive, that would do anything to win.

Another gunshot rang out, this one muffled. Then the attacker was standing over me again, blocking my view of the sun.

He was broad shouldered with round goggles on, like pilots of those old-fashioned crop dusters wear, with some kind of close-fitting helmet on his head. He was pointing the gun at me again. The prone form of Evan Saunders was in my peripheral vision. I smelled the iron tang of blood mixed with dust.

I knew he was dead, that he had died for me.

The knowing twisted in me like a knife.

I looked at him, for just a moment. He was on his back, his head pointed toward me, his legs splayed out awkwardly. I saw his empty, slitted eyes. Blood was still leaking from his chest and staining his dark clothing.

There was another scream, animalistic and primal. This time the scream didn't come from our attacker, it came from me.

I abandoned the peace of meditation and let my anger drive me to a different place in my mind. A more primal place. A desperate place.

The quality of my scream changed into something with a vague metallic edge as my grey prison jumpsuit began burning, as the man above me fired his gun, as the bullet passed through my neutrino form without hurting me, as I rose to my feet and leapt onto my attacker, the two of us going down in a jumble.

I was on top of him, not really knowing what had happened. My fist connected with his cheek and his skin sizzled away. He grunted, both of his gloved fists connecting with my chest. I went flying back and landed in the debris of the building.

"That's better," he said as he rose to his feet. I gawked as I watched the ragged ground-beef wound on his face heal itself. He was a q-morph. He was trying to kill me. Why?

He was dressed in rugged black clothing, with dull black armor over most of his body. His chest, his arms, his legs. His skull was covered with a sleek black helmet and his eyes covered by those aviator goggles. He had a thick belt at his waste that held several gun holsters, some small round devices, and some other pouches. His jaw was set, his mouth a thin, grim line. Honestly, he reminded me of Batman, but without the cape and with silly goggles.

He took one of the round black objects from his belt and threw it at me before running to my right.

I surged up into the air as the object landed on the rubble of the building and exploded. The explosion was small, hardly noticeable. And then a dark purple energy ball erupted from it, expanding rapidly. The energy ball quickly engulfed my legs as I flew upward. My legs went numb and I fell to a heap onto the brick rubble.

An energy grenade. I had never seen one of these before. It had to be something new created by the aliens. He was a q-morph and working for the aliens. It made no sense.

I sat up, my legs useless, and fired neutrino bolts at the running soldier. One of them clipped his leg and he went down.

"Why are you trying to kill me?" I shouted.

He slowly got up and smiled, his left hand going to his belt, his right hand grasping a gun.

"Why?" I repeated.

I hated that I couldn't see his eyes. Just like the guards down in the prison with the dark sunglasses. None of the guards had worn them as they escorted me out, as they fought and died to protect my life. They had finally been human to me. This soldier was not.

He threw another grenade at me and instinctively I extended both of my hands, and a yellow beam of neutronic energy stabbed out from my chest and formed a shield in front of me. The grenade sizzled when it hit the shield, the purple energy ball bursting from it. My shield sputtered out, consumed by the energy ball, but it didn't touch me this time.

I fired neutrino bolts at my attacker as he ran around the rubble that I sat on. He threw grenades at me two more times and I managed to block them with my neutrino shield. Each time the shield was smaller, and I was left feeling an exhaustion I had never known. My neutrino bolts became weak and anemic. I felt my reaction nearing failure.

He sensed this and stopped running and walked slowly towards me. A gun in his right hand, an energy grenade in his left.

"Why?" I asked again. I considered flying away, but my legs were still numb and I didn't think I had the energy for it.

"You're in the way," he said. His voice was even, all that running and he didn't seem the least bit tired.

"Of what?"

"Of the future," he said with a smile.

I laughed. I'm in the way of the future? What the hell kind of cryptic bullshit was that? His smile turned into a sour frown. He didn't like to be laughed at.

No more talking, he threw the grenade at me. This one, I noticed, was bigger than the last few had been. His aim was good, it was going to connect directly with me.

I didn't try to throw up a shield, I didn't think it was in me, but rolled awkwardly over the rubble away from where I had been sitting.

My legs were not strong, but I had just a touch of control of them and I was doing a strange log-roll down the pile of rubble when the grenade hit. This grenade was different. It sent out a ball of energy and then exploded for real, not a small explosion like the others.

He had waited until I was drained to throw this one. It was meant to strip me of power with the energy portion of it and kill me with the concussive portion of it.

The purple energy ball expanded rapidly, clipping my right arm as I rolled away, but I retained my form. The concussive component of it threw me and the rubble I was rolling on into the air.

Time slowed.

I was flying in the air, still doing my log-roll spin. My head was facing the soldier, my arms close to my body, my palms facing him. His left arm was still extended from his throw, his face grim and determined.

I knew there wasn't much left in me. I had been through too much today. I had turned twice without a charge. I knew I would be lucky to hold my neutrino form for even a few more seconds.

I tweaked the position of my palms and fired neutrino bolts from both of them.

In this slowed-down state, they erupted slowly and flew gracefully through the air towards my attacker, scintillating yellow balls of energy. Four in total, two from each palm.

All four were well aimed. All four plowed into his chest and burned their way through his armor and into his flesh.

And that was all the energy I had, my neutrino form fading as I fell.

33 / COERCED?

MY NAKED FLESH CONNECTED WITH THE HARD GROUND NEAR Groom Lake, rubble raining down on me, pain lancing through my body. All four neutrino bolts had hit the goggled soldier's chest. He should be dead. But I didn't think I was safe.

As the dust settled, I assessed my condition. I was dizzy and weak, a spiking pain in my head, I had lots of scrapes and blossoming bruises. My body hurt all over, but nothing seemed to be broken. I thought of staring up at the sun again, trying to trigger another change, but if the soldier survived, I didn't have time for that.

I raised my head and looked around. The soldier was lying still on the ground about ten yards away. The corpse of one of my guards was lying a few feet from me. The brown-haired one that always had the pole with the cuffs on it. I saw blood on his face and then noticed the gun on his belt. And the Taser.

I crawled over. I thought that if I stood, I would just fall down. As I did, I heard a groan from the q-morph soldier. He wasn't dead. He was going to attack again.

My mouth and throat were parched and dry. I was desperate for water. My stomach gnawed with hunger. I needed sleep. Crawling that six feet seemed more like climbing a mountain. When I got to him the first thing I took was his Taser. I pointed it at my chest and fired, the two metal connectors embedding themselves into my flesh, the voltage stored in the device pouring into my body.

Lightningirl wasn't here. I needed some kind of power.

My muscles contracted briefly as the energy flowed into me, but only briefly. My body recognized it for what it was and opened up to it.

I didn't feel good, but I felt a little better. I heard a scrape from behind me, grabbed my guard's gun, and still lying on the ground, turned.

The soldier made it to his feet, the hole in his chest closing itself up as he moved. "Much better," he grunted with a grin. "I'd have hated it for this to be easy."

I must have looked pitiful lying there naked with my stomach sucked in, my body ravaged from my long fast and my repeated transformations, my hands shaking as I pointed the gun at him.

"It'll be quick now," he said as he stood all the way up. "I promise."

I took a deep breath, pushing away the yammering of my mind. *You're going to die. Now. You will never see Licia again. He's one of them. This means the aliens are coming back. They will succeed. The planet will fall. You will fail.*

It wasn't a meditation, at least not like I had done it before. I remained fully aware of my surroundings, but I was following my breath, letting my thoughts go as they bubbled up.

"Leave now," I slowly said, "and I won't kill you." My voice seemed to come from far away in this semi-meditative state.

He laughed, his voice deep and rumbling. The sound of the approaching helicopter was getting louder, but if he didn't have senses like I did, I doubted that he could hear it yet. "Kind, you are," he said, "but I think I'll take this chance."

His hand went to his side and the gun holstered there. I fired, aiming for his chest. I knew how a gun worked, I knew how to fire one, but I wasn't very good at it. Guns had never interested me.

As I fired, I reached down and found my own trigger. To survive I had to. There was no time. I had the tiny boost from the Taser and with all my heart believed it was possible.

Most of my bullets missed, but one clipped him in the right shoulder and he hesitated for just a moment. By then I was Neutrinoman and standing in front of him.

He held up his hands away from his body, his mouth opening and closing in surprise or maybe fear. With his eyes behind those goggles it was hard to tell.

"The aliens... they've... they've got my son," he stammered, his deep voice sounding suddenly weak. "My wife. They're going to kill them if I don't kill you."

Part of me loved what he was telling me. That there was a reason a q-morph was trying to kill me, was working with the aliens. Another part of me didn't believe a word of it.

"What are their names? Where are they being held? Tell me everything you know and I'll do what I can."

"No," he said, his voice shaking now. "They're monitoring us. Right now. I..." His left hand was drifting slowly down.

I extended one arm, palm forward. "Get your hand back up or I will fire at you until there is nothing left." It was an empty threat. I didn't have that kind of energy.

He nodded as I heard the sound of sirens in the distance as well as the thump-thump of a helicopter. The cavalry was coming. All I needed to do was keep him here until they arrived.

"Tell me something about yourself," I said. It felt like the most awkward question in the world as I stood there, but I wanted to know he was real. Was human. I was looking for a reason not to kill him. I *needed* a reason not to kill him.

"What?" he asked, looking around as if my question was some sort if lame diversion.

"You know," I said with a nod, "if we met at a party, what would you tell me so I knew something about you. Who you are as a person?"

"Are you mad?" he asked. "I just tried to kill you. I just told you my wife's and child's lives hang in balance."

I shrugged. "We've got a few minutes. Tell me something about yourself."

His forehead furrowed deeply above the goggles. "Umm... I like to play checkers. My dad started teaching me when I was four years old. Still like to play."

I smiled. There it was—he was a real person now. Not just my enemy.

"Is your father gone?" I asked.

He nodded, a sly grin blooming on his face. "He is, as you will be too soon."

I was confused for a moment. Did he just threaten to kill me again? He shuffled his feet awkwardly, first his right heel tapping against his left and then he slammed his right heel into the ground.

A purple energy ball erupted from the heel of his left boot and engulfed both of us. My neutrino form fled, I collapsed onto the ground.

I knew it was time to die and my thoughts were all of Licia. I could see her face in my mind's eye again, her beautiful round face. Her coffee with cream skin. Her thick expressive eyebrows. Her deep brown eyes.

All the parts went together again. It wasn't much, but I clung to it.

A shot rang out and I tensed, but nothing happened. I heard the soldier grunt in pain and heard his retreating boots. The cavalry was here.

I was going to survive.

I unceremoniously passed out.

SUMMER 2025, CASITA DE SOLEDAD, CENTRAL ARIZONA

THE RADIUS OF THE ALIEN ENERGY EXPLOSION WAS MASSIVE AT our home of exile in the high desert of Arizona. It was the kind that didn't harm physical matter, but before I knew it was on me and Licia. It stripped me of my power and I was then naked and we were both falling.

It was one of the purple energy balls designed for me, not the orange ones that worked on her. This was why she wouldn't leave me, even though I asked her to. This was why she put up with the aerial acrobatics, even though she hated it so. She worried it would be like this.

As we fell, I felt her feeding me electricity. I saw the arc of lightning she drew from the nearby high-tension power lines.

We had about seven seconds before we hit the ground. She would survive as Lightningirl, I would not if I was still flesh and blood.

We were out of practice. We didn't train or do drills anymore. We made the occasional trip to orbit to piss off Homeland Security, but that was about it.

We tumbled and fell. Lightningirl fed me power. I changed several seconds before we hit the ground and thrust us upwards, but it wasn't enough.

We slammed into the ground hard in the bottom of the blackened pit that our excavation had turned into, the bomb, Project Vulcan, still buried beneath us.

I looked down, but the sight had fled, I couldn't see what was going on. I got up, grabbed Lightningirl and flew us low over the ground away from the bomb. We didn't get far before an orange energy ball engulfed us and suddenly Licia was flesh in my arms and screaming.

When she's Lightningirl, my energy can charge her up, just as hers can charge me up. When she's flesh and blood, my neutronic touch is destructive.

We were flying low over the ground and I dropped her. She hit hard and rolled awkwardly, the desert biting at her bare flesh. I landed in front of her, trying to look away from her damaged flesh, the red and blistered areas where I had been touching her, but I couldn't.

I didn't get us very far from the bomb, maybe one hundred yards. Licia cursed, reached out her left hand and drew a lightning bolt from the high-tension power lines and was back to being Lightningirl.

"I really want to hurt someone now," she said.

The bomb was made for us. They knew us and how we worked together.

"Thank God for the power lines," I said. I was looking towards them when the explosion occurred. It didn't come from the bomb, but from the tower closest to us. It was a small explosion, but enough to take out the tower. The giant metal structure began to screech as the metal bent and broke, as it fell, as power lines snapped, as Lightningirl was cut off from her power supply.

I opened my mouth to say something when the next purple

energy ball erupted, followed several seconds later by an orange energy ball.

Licia and I were left naked and without a power source. My uranium was gone, her electricity supply had been destroyed.

It was the end, I knew it. We had a good life, we had each other. But just because it's the end, doesn't mean you stop fighting. I grabbed her hand and we started running naked through the desert away from the bomb.

They had stripped us of our power, and we both knew it was time for the "vulcan" part of Project Vulcan.

35 / LICIA

Licia was holding me there in the desert of Area 51, on the rubble of the structure that had been the entryway to my prison. I was so glad that I think I wept. But I can't be sure, it's all fuzzy. My body had been through so much I was having trouble holding onto consciousness.

I heard sirens and the loud thrash of a landing helicopter, felt the hard ground underneath me, my mouth tasting of dust and blood. And then I felt her arms, the electric tingle of her touch, heard her voice. "I'm here, Nik. I'm here."

I opened my eyes, just a bit, and saw her face haloed by the sunlight. When she's Lightningirl, she looks like a goddess. That day she was an angel.

"God, you're beautiful," I said, my voice much weaker than I expected it to be.

She laughed nervously. "And you're a mess. What happened?"

I heard the baritone bark of Colonel Williams giving orders, boots scraping the ground, questions asked of me, but I only had eyes and ears for Licia.

"Attacked by a q-morph soldier. I need... to..."

"Save it, Nichols," Williams said, his lean, angular face entering my field of view next to Licia's, the light haloing him too. "This is no time for a debrief. You need medical attention first."

Williams's face was no longer in my field of vision and I heard him barking more orders. Something about securing the area.

Licia leaned close, her lips tickling my ear. "We have a plan. We won't be here long." She pulled away, but I signaled with my hand for her to come close. "What?" she asked, her breath smelling sweet.

"Pot roast," I said, uttering the agreed upon words when we had parted after the destruction of the Hoover Dam. Pot Roast, the meal my mother served the day I met Licia.

She pulled back, smiled, and nodded, and then the smile faded and tears were running down her face. She wiped them off and held a water bottle to my lips and I drank in huge gulps and ended up coughing most of it up.

Next thing I knew, I was in a jeep with a blanket wrapped around me, Licia still holding me. We were speeding across Groom Lake. Colonel Williams was driving.

"Is he well enough?" he asked, his head darting back to the two of us.

"Nik, can you hear me?" Licia shouted.

I nodded.

"I want to get you off this base. There's a vehicle waiting. Are you well enough to leave right away?"

I looked at her and smiled. The worry in her eyes was sobering. "All I need is you, my love," I said.

Licia snorted and turned to Williams. "He's fine. Get us the hell out of here."

THE RV WAS LONG AND BLACK AND PERFECTLY POLISHED. IT

looked so out of place sitting on the narrow blacktop in the middle of the Nevada desert in front of the gate into Area 51.

It took both Williams and Licia to get me out of the jeep and headed towards the RV. I was not in good shape. I was weak, dehydrated, bruised, and battered.

After we got past the gate, two figures got out of the RV. A tall, middle-aged man in a black suit, the driver, and Jennifer Johnson, dressed in shorts and a blue T-shirt instead of her usual lab coat, with her nerd glasses on and her curly black hair pulled into a semblance of a ponytail.

Jennifer rushed over and took me away from Williams and Licia. We all stood there for a moment. I was trying to assimilate all of this.

"Will you be okay?" Licia asked Williams, her eyes straying back to the gate with its tall fencing, barbed wire, and guard's house.

He grunted and nodded his head. "You're both civilians. You asked to leave. I was following protocol."

A tear ran down Licia's cheek as she stood on her tiptoes and kissed him on his cheek. "Thank you," she whispered.

Williams blushed, his cheeks turning bright red. He quickly walked back to the jeep and drove back into the base.

"What is this?" I asked Licia, looking at the RV.

"It's a long story," she said. "One not suited to our current surroundings."

"Let's get you fixed up," Jennifer said, she and Licia and the driver helping me into the RV.

As Licia and I ran away from the next stage of Project Vulcan, fully human and naked, I kept thinking, *we've been through worse.* I thought it as my foot grazed a prickly pear cactus, as I fell and rocks bit into my bare flesh, as Licia went down and cried out.

But there was no time for thought. Only running. Only making sure Licia was with me, that I was touching her.

Our bodies didn't do their usual energy exchange. We were tapped. I noticed this too and pushed the thought away. I went back to my breath. I needed the oxygen to run.

Just my breath. Just the physical exertion. Just the touch of Licia. That was enough to keep me moving over the dry, rough land. That was all there was. That was my world.

The end comes to us all, even superheroes. I pushed that thought away too.

Just the breath. Just the run. Just Licia.

We didn't look back, only forward. We knew the threat was

there, no need to slow ourselves down imagining we'll see the explosion coming for us and somehow be able to outrun it.

Just the breath. Just the run. Just Licia.

My eyes slitted from fatigue. My lungs burning from the effort. Most of my mind in service of this moment, this need, this now. It wasn't a meditation, not how I had learned it, but running can be meditative.

And there it was, the trigger deep inside of me, the one I learned of in prison.

"Stop!" I yelled as I flipped that switch, as I drew from my internal reserves to once again become Neutrinoman.

Time slowed. I felt the earth rumbling beneath me. "Get down!"

I turned towards it. I extended both my hands in a defensive gesture. The beam of yellow extended from my chest and formed a shield in front of us.

The earth was disintegrating as the wave of energy hit the shield. I willed the shield into a sphere around Licia and me. The blast of energy parted at the shield and went around us, under us, disintegrating the earth below us.

I recognized this blast. I first saw it in prison when the two guards with energy weapons shot each other and were vaporized. Project Vulcan used two pieces of alien technology: the energy balls to strip our powers and the energy bomb to reduce us to atoms. They had somehow reproduced what happened in the prison, an alien energy ball hitting an alien energy source and vaporizing everything in its sphere.

We fell, the earth below us gone, the blast of energy past us, the earth all around us just gone. My spherical shield held. We were standing on normal earth inside the shield as it fell straight down like Wile E. Coyote falling off of a cliff in a Road Runner cartoon.

The epicenter of the bomb was far below the surface and it vaporized a spherical area about two hundred yards around it. We were near the edge of the blast radius far above the bomb, which left us with a long way to fall. Too far.

"You've got to change!" I yelled as we fell.

I stood in the middle of our little sphere with the neutrino shield still around us. Licia was off center and that imbalance in weight caused our sphere to tip. I was going to tumble into her.

But I was Neutrinoman, and unlike when we were flying, she had time. Not much, but some time. She thrust out her left hand, I felt her drawing power from me like she can from plants, people, or rampaging buffalo. The natural tendency of our bodies to feed each other was intensified by her will, yellow tendrils of energy flowing from me to her. I let the shield go, the dirt below our feet crumbling, and we fell into the empty space beneath us as she pulled energy from me.

It seemed like it took forever, although I know it was only a few seconds. I didn't thrust, I fell with her, and at the last moment she changed.

We hit the ground hard and tumbled to the bottom of the sphere.

THE RV WAS RIGGED FOR MEDICAL INTERVENTION. A HEART monitor, IV stand, even a defibrillator. I don't remember too much about those first few hours. Jennifer examined me, got me on to a bed, and hooked me to the IV. Licia fed me. I faded in and out of consciousness.

I felt terrible, but I was so grateful to be away from that prison, to be free of my interrogator, to be with people I cared about.

"I love you both," I mumbled once as consciousness began to fade again. I don't know if they heard me. I don't know if they replied. It didn't matter.

And then I was back in the prison in my grey jumpsuit, pacing my twelve-by-twelve cell, experiencing the colors and textures that I knew so well, my fingers touching the books on the shelf. I worried that I had dreamed that they had let me go, that I had had that battle with the q-morph soldier, that I was with Licia and Jennifer.

My little bookshelf was there with a few novels and my meditation book. I took the meditation book and went to my spot in the middle of the cell. My wool blanket was already there and folded up properly. I sat cross-legged and didn't open the book, just held it, looking at the cover with the tree and the mountaintop peeking out of the mist, letting my breath slide in and out of my lungs.

My thoughts were so clear. The real prison was inside. It didn't matter if Licia and Jennifer and the soldier were a dream or if this was a dream. I had the key. My breath was the way. It was all so simple.

"It's important you keep meditating," Ronald said, a smile on his kind face as he stood at the door to my cell.

"I hate it," I replied. "It's hard. Does it ever get easy?"

He shook his head. "Not really. It's not supposed to be easy."

I nodded and remembered what Larry, my interrogator, had said about him, those videos he showed of me reading a book that wasn't there.

"Are you real?" I asked.

He smiled. "One hundred percent," he said. "But I was never in this prison."

"What?" I asked. "How?"

He tapped his head with his index finger.

"You're a q-morph," I said.

He smiled. "That I am."

"So I'm not crazy," I said, a goofy grin on my face. "I just had a q-morph making me see things that weren't there."

Ronald's brow wrinkled. "Oh, everything you saw exists. I do, those books do. Reality isn't such a black and white thing."

I was dreaming, I knew it then. This was a dream of Ronald, my mind trying to make sense of what I had experienced. Giving me a story that would make it so I wouldn't think myself crazy.

Ronald took a deep breath and sighed. "You are dreaming, but you are not making this up. You didn't make me up."

I got up and opened the gate to my cell. It was a dream. I could do what I wanted. "Prove it."

Ronald shrugged his shoulders. "If I must."

We walked down the bland hallway past the door to the interrogation room, around a corner, to another door. I had never been in this door. He opened it and waved me to enter. In it was my interrogator, Evan Saunders, and another guard.

"His name isn't Larry," Ronald said, indicating my interrogator. He was seated at a desk with a large LCD monitor and a microphone. On the monitor I saw myself handcuffed to a chair in the middle of the interrogation room. "His name is Christopher Halifax. He used to work for the CIA and then did some black ops for a while. He lives in Laguna Beach, California, is on his third wife, has three kids and five grandkids." Ronald then proceeded to tell me his address, the name of all of his children, the address of the gym he uses when he's home, and a bunch of other things.

"Why are you telling me all this?" I asked.

"You wanted proof," he shrugged. "This is it. When you wake up, check it out. You'll find that every piece of it is correct."

I stood there staring at the scene. Ronald, my interrogator, Evan who died saving my life. I found myself believing him.

And then something clicked in my head. "You work for Tom Tyree." That first book Ronald had given me had a note from Tom in it. The book hadn't been there in my hands. Ronald had projected it into my mind.

Ronald smiled, his cheeks rising high. "Kind of. I'm not part of his gang, if that's what you think. I just owed him a favor."

I nodded. This time Tom's intervention didn't disturb me at all. I had needed Ronald.

"What's next?" I asked.

Ronald shrugged. "You get yourself better. You keep yourself away from the military. You save the world."

I groaned.

"Hell of a burden, isn't it, kid?" he asked, clapping me on the back.

I nodded.

"One more thing," he said as he turned and left the room,

looking at me over his shoulder. "You've got an offer coming your way. You're not going to like it, but keep an open mind."

I tried to ask Ronald another question, but he was gone.

⊏⊐

"WHERE ARE WE?" I ASKED. I HAD SLEPT FOR WHAT FELT LIKE days, but we were still rumbling along in that fancy black RV. My mouth tasted like old socks and I was horribly weak but getting better. I had woken up in the bedroom in the back of the RV, managed to get myself to the little bathroom and walked up to the front. Out the window I saw desert and cactus that seemed to go on forever.

A tall man dressed in a black suit was driving, and Jennifer and Licia were seated at the little table towards the front. They both had laptops out.

"Mexico," Licia said with a smile. "Feeling better?"

I nodded and eased my body down next to her, a few tendrils of electricity jumping from her body to mine. No yellow neutronic energy jumped back—I still wasn't right. "Whose RV is this? Who's the driver?"

Jennifer smiled. "A gift from a fan." She reached across the table and put two fingers to my neck, checking my pulse.

"His name isn't Tom Tyree, is it?"

Licia shook her head. "No. Why do you ask?"

I shrugged, remembering my dream of Ronald. "That guy just keeps showing up. So, who's the fan?"

Licia took my hand and smiled. "Let's just wait on that. He'll be down to meet you when you're feeling a bit better."

"He's got an offer to make me, doesn't he?" I asked. The widening of the ladies' eyes told me I was on the right track. "And I'm not going to like it, am I?"

Licia shook her head, her silky hair sliding across her shoulders. God, that woman is beautiful. I laughed. It wasn't about humor, but relief. That was enough. I knew Ronald and the dream were real. I knew that I hadn't been imagining all of it.

I knew there was more to do, more to know, but I needed rest. A lot more rest.

I slowly got back up. "Help me back?" I said to Licia.

She smiled and nodded, letting me lean on her as we made our way back to the bedroom in the back of the RV.

"You okay?" she asked.

"I will be," I said, and I believed it.

WINTER 2005, SONORA, MEXICO

I HEALED SLOWLY, AND THAT WAS FINE BY ME. NO NUCLEAR reactor to help me out, only time, the sun, and gentle infusions of electricity from Lightningirl.

I've lived inland all my life, and after two weeks in Mexico by the beach I had come to love the water and the sun and the wonderful white noise of the ocean. The driver—his name was Valentine Oscar—had driven us across the border, past Rocky Point, and a few hours farther south to an empty stretch of beach with a little adobe casita.

He was more than a driver. He was bodyguard, cook, and companion to us. Another gift from my benefactor. My initial impression of him was terribly wrong. A middle-aged man in a black suit that drives vehicles for a living. It was a small description to capture the quiet, complicated man. Val was a gourmet cook, a martial arts expert, and also a very gentle man.

Well, I suspect he hasn't always been gentle, he carried a gun too. Maybe I should rephrase that. He was clearly a man capable of doing great damage and interacted with the world all that much more gently because of it.

I learned a lot by watching him.

In those two weeks we became something of a family. Jennifer was motherly, making me take vitamins, drink a lot of water, and constantly checking my vitals. Val was like a quiet father, watching over us all, attending to our physical safety. Licia and I, we were... We were in love, of course, but more than that, we had finally been through enough to get truly comfortable with each other.

I was happy. I was glad to be alive. I was with the love of my life and my best friend and making a new friend. I wasn't saving the world or fighting for my life. I wasn't dealing with the military or psychopathic super-villains. And, most importantly, I wasn't in prison.

It was idyllic except for the dreams. Every night I would be back in my cell alone, or back on the metal chair, the voice of my interrogator my only company.

On our thirteenth night there, it was particularly bad. I woke up, my body covered in sweat, crying out, ripping the covers from my body like it was trying to smother me.

"Honey, honey," Licia said, trying to hold me, but I shook her off. "It's okay. You're fine. You're with me."

My body shook with fear and I let her hold me until the shaking died down.

"I'm never going back," I finally said, my words thick, my throat raw.

"To the States?" she asked.

I nodded. "Can we stay here? What does this benefactor expect from us?" We still hadn't talked about it. I had been content to let time slide by pleasantly and avoid such realities.

The white noise of the Sea of Cortez floated in through the cracked window, the room simple and not much larger than the queen-sized bed. It had a dresser made of old wood and side-tables that were antique trunks.

"You can ask him when you meet him," Licia said.

"When is that?" I asked.

"I told him you would need at least two weeks," she said, her hand caressing my neck.

"I need more time than that," I said quietly.

"Okay. I'll call him tomorrow."

"Who is he?" I asked.

The curtains were open. I always had to have them open to not feel like I was trapped. The night was dark and the room was only vague shapes. In the darkness, I felt her shrug.

I was out of the bed before I knew it, looking around, my breath coming in ragged gasps. She didn't know who had given us these gifts. What would they want from me?

There was a soft knock on the door. "Is everything okay, Mr. Nichols?" Valentine asked.

I jumped. Who was Valentine, really? What would he do if I didn't cooperate with this benefactor?

I moved towards the window, it looked out over a dark expanse of beach, the Gulf of Mexico beyond.

Could we get away?

"Nik had another bad dream," Licia said. "We're fine, Val."

"Let me know if you need anything," he said.

"We will," Licia replied. "Thank you."

Licia joined me at the window, her arms resting on my shoulder, the tingle of our energy exchange starting to calm me.

"You don't know who he is?" I asked.

"Not really, no," she said, worry leaking into her voice.

"Then why?" I asked.

"He knew they were releasing you," she said. "Williams confirmed it. He knew you'd be a mess and would need to leave right away. He presented me with this plan. I had to do something. I..."

"It's okay," I said.

We were silent for a long time. She wrapped her arms around

me as I stared out the window onto the beach lit in the ghostly light of the moon. It doesn't get that cold down here in the winter, the nighttime temperatures in the high fifties. The window was cracked and the light breeze flowed through, the sound of the waves soothed my fearful mind.

I let myself slip into a semi-meditative state. The warmth of Licia's body against mine, the cool of the breeze, the gentle in and out of my breath. I hadn't tried to meditate since I had gotten out of prison—it had seemed like something that belonged in the past too. But there I slipped into it quickly and easily.

Minutes slid past and then my sight changed. I could see the blue lines of electricity in Licia's hands where they gripped me. A pulsing vibrant blue much brighter than I had seen from the guards in the prison. I turned and looked at her. It was like I could see Lightningirl beneath the flesh. It was there, hidden, ready. She said something, but I was somewhere else, somewhere where talking didn't matter.

I smiled and looked around the room.

I saw a trickling blue line of electricity snaking through the wall and cord to the alarm clock on our bed. Through one wall I could see the faint blue tracery outline of Jennifer asleep in her bed in the room next to us.

I looked carefully around the room looking for anything else that consumed electricity. A cell phone in Licia's purse. A charging laptop on the little wooden dresser. I went out into the living room and kitchen and looked there too. The clock on the stove. The flat-screen TV. Nothing strange, nothing unusual. Through another door I could see the electrical charge of Valentine asleep.

Licia was worried. I wasn't acting normal. I hadn't even gotten dressed, only pulling on a robe. She spoke to me again and I gave her a smile and signaled for her to follow me.

I couldn't speak. That would destroy the mental state I was in. When she hesitated, I took her hand and gently pulled her out of the house.

It was an adobe structure with a flat roof and rounded edges. Simple and lovely. Our refuge. It greatly influenced us when we built Casita de Soledad.

I walked slowly around the house looking for anything that might be a hidden camera or listening device and I couldn't find any.

By the time I was done, Valentine was out with us, keeping back several yards, but shadowing our every move.

I ignored him and led Licia down to the beach.

"What is it? Are you okay?" she asked. I had been silent long enough that she was very worried.

"I'm fine," I said quietly, letting myself come back to a more normal level of consciousness. I was sad to see the inner Lightningirl fade away as my meditative state fled.

"Really?" she asked, her arms folded. "What the hell was that?"

I hadn't told her very much about my time in prison, about what I had learned, what I could do.

"It's a long story," I said. "Do you have a few hours?"

She smiled and nodded.

"But first things first. In the morning, call this benefactor. Tell him I'm ready to see him now."

SUMMER 2025, CASITA DE SOLEDAD, CENTRAL ARIZONA

CASITA DE SOLEDAD WAS GONE. THE LAND WAS GONE. IN ITS place was this huge, bizarre sphere of hollowed out earth that was melted and blackened at its edges. The alien bomb vaporized everything in its path.

"You okay?" I grunted after we stopped moving.

"Alive," she grunted back.

Our limbs were tangled together and all I could see was the blue sky above us framed by the eerily round sphere.

I started laughing. Not that there was anything funny about this. Our home destroyed. Our future unknown. It was more the stress.

"What's so damn funny?" Lightningirl asked as she stood up and looked around.

"Nothing," I said, trying to suppress my laughter.

"No, really," she said, her hands on her hips. "I'd like to hear what is amusing you right now. I could use a good laugh."

Her electrical face was serious. I knew I shouldn't be laughing, but I just couldn't help it. I got myself briefly under control and stood up, but then descended back into a gale of laughter.

Lightningirl wasn't talking anymore. She was staring at me, hands still on her cocked hips.

"I'm sorry," I said. "Really. This isn't funny. It's ridiculous. We've been living with this damn bomb under us the whole time. Look at what it did." I pointed to the smooth curved earth around us two hundred yards in diameter.

She pursed her lips. "And this is funny, why? What the hell are we going to do now? We have no home. No possessions. Nothing. Homeland Security will be here shortly to see if we survived. And when they find us, I don't think it will be all that pleasant."

The world doesn't want its heroes when it's done with them. Not when those heroes are powerful and dangerous. The world wants us to do our deed, to save them, and then just disappear.

"Well, at least you have me," I offered, trying to put a genuine smile on my face. She had told me that was all she wanted.

"For that I am grateful," she said with a small smile. "But, seriously, what are we going to do now?"

"We do what we always do," I said. "We survive."

She nodded and started pacing. As you might have noticed reading these memoirs, I'm happy to wing it. Not Licia, she wants to have a plan.

I let her pace. I figured we had a little time before Homeland showed up. They had clearly been caught off guard by all of this. She paced around me, our bodies close enough to do their energy dance, thin yellow and blue-white tendrils arching between us.

After several minutes she stopped. "Diane Madison," she said.

"What?" I asked.

"Our interview with her is in just over two weeks," she said.

"So?"

She stared at me. "Live TV, Nik. We can make our case to the people. We just need a place to hide out until then, and we need evidence of what happened here, like some video footage."

I smiled. "Not only are you beautiful, you're smart too. I know who can help us get that footage, but I haven't a clue as to where we go."

"I have a place," she said shyly looking down, the comment not really registering with me.

"So there we go," I said. "A plan."

Licia nodded and came into my arms and I held her tight, feeling the increased energy of our q-morph forms close together.

"We'll get through this," I whispered. "Together."

"Promise?" she asked.

"I promise."

I then flew us out of the empty sphere that used to be our high desert home. The change I had feared and also wanted was now upon us. Our sheltered, small life was over, never to return. One way or another, things were going to be very different from now on.

I flew us low over the rolling desert landscape towards sanctuary, towards our unknown future.

OUR LITTLE ADOBE CASITA IN MEXICO, WHERE I HEALED UP from my imprisonment, had a flagstone patio out behind it with a fine view of the ocean. On it was a black metal table and four chairs, the metal faded from wind, sun, and weather.

Valentine stood a few steps away watching us and our surroundings. I had asked him to sit, but he had refused. On my right was Licia and on my left was Jennifer.

We were all dressed for our location, looking like expats glad to be away from the stress of the States. Loose clothing, T-shirts or loose short-sleeved shirts, shorts or loose pants, all of it in one earth tone or another.

Across from me sat our benefactor.

He was short, maybe forty, with short brown hair that was making a quick retreat from his forehead. He was a bit overweight and his hands were always in motion. Rubbing the worn metal of the table, playing with the buttons of his white silk shirt, fiddling with his sunglasses.

There had been introductions, thank yous from us for his hospitality, and small talk. His name was Aaron Jordan.

"Shall we get started?" he asked as he reached into his briefcase that sat on the flagstone beside him.

"I have a question first," I said.

"Sure," he said, fiddling with his buttons again.

"Actually, a request and then a question," I said. He nodded. "Can you take off your sunglasses and tell me to exactly what extent Tom Tyree is involved in all of this."

His brow furrowed above his dark glasses. Under the table Licia squeezed my hand and Jennifer glanced at me and gave me a small nod. We had all talked about this approach.

"I'll know if you're lying," Licia told him, although it was a lie. "Both of us have new abilities emerging."

"And I'm sure Tom told you how much I value the truth," I added. "So you wouldn't even think of lying."

Aaron smiled and nodded as he took off his glasses, his light brown eyes meeting mine. "Tom did tell me that, and he has played a catalytic role here, but he's no longer involved."

"Why?" Jennifer asked.

Aaron smiled. I think he was enjoying the exchange. "This doesn't work with him involved. He's too much of a villain, and what we want to do is gather the heroes."

"It's a fine line between the two," I said, remembering how things had changed so abruptly for me after the Hoover Dam.

"That it is," he said. "For some, but not for you. You will always be a hero."

The word rubbed me the wrong way. I knew that I was considered a hero, a superhero, but the word seemed to hide the hard realities of having power and trying to do the right thing with it. But I let the comment go by. I didn't want to engage on morals or ethics. I wanted to get to the offer that Ronald told me I wouldn't like but should listen to.

"And what is it that you want from us?" I asked.

He pulled three glossy blue folders from his briefcase and handed one to each of us. On the cover was a round embossed logo that said, "Heroes Incorporated."

I almost groaned. The word "hero" was not something I liked or even understood anymore.

"It's pretty simple," Aaron began. "We have commitments of money, property, and services to start an organization for both of you and for the other heroes. A place where you can meet this alien threat without the burden of the military. An organization that will work with the military but not be controlled by them. Where you can set your own course, defend this planet, your own way."

He stood up and started pacing over the flagstone, his hands animated, his voice gaining strength. "I have commitments of five hundred million dollars to start this. If you sign on, I can triple that in a week. We can gather the q-morphs, train them, get them all the resources they need. We can meet this threat with our eyes open. This will be your organization to run as you see fit."

My mind was still stuck on "five hundred million dollars." That was a huge amount of money. What would I possibly need all that for? And how would we go about defending the planet from the aliens? How could that amount of money make a difference?

I was vaguely aware of the rustling of papers as Licia and Jennifer opened their folders.

"...as you'll see on this spreadsheet," he continued, "I've set up a preliminary budget. Most of it in creating a lab, hiring staff, creating a secure base of operations. I think if—"

"Wait," I said, holding up my hand.

Aaron stopped his hand in the air, his mouth open, a surprised look on his face. "Is there a problem?"

"Back up. Five hundred million dollars?"

He nodded. "Yes, not all cash. Some of it is services. We have offers of land too."

"What's wrong?" Licia asked.

"That's a crazy amount of money," I said. "Why would they

give us that much? What do they want from us?" The military spent tens of millions on me, I knew it. Taking over part of Palo Verde, training me, hiring people like Jennifer to deal with health and other concerns, flying me all over the place. And what had they wanted? For me to shut up and color in the lines. What would these people want that were planning on giving us hundreds of millions of dollars?

Aaron sat back in his chair and leaned towards me. "These companies are the biggest on the planet: Wal-Mart, GM, Apple, Google, Tesla, Amazon. There are only three small stipulations that come with the money. First, that the organization be called Heroes Incorporated; second, that you are the head of the organization; and third, that their involvement be public knowledge." He paused, taking a deep breath. "But what they really want, Mr. Nichols, is for you to save us. Not one dollar that they have matters if we don't survive."

My heart started thumping in my chest, an insistent and loud knock. The gentle crashing of the ocean suddenly seemed a roar. Aaron was talking, but I couldn't hear him anymore. Why was it always me that had to save the planet? All I wanted, all I had ever wanted, was love and work worth doing. I never wanted to be a hero. I never wanted to have to save anyone let alone the entire planet.

I didn't want this.

Aaron was talking, telling me it wasn't a rush, that they could start much of it without me, that I could stay here a while longer, but I couldn't really hear him. I surged up, knocking the chair down and stumbled past the patio and out onto the hot sand. I needed to be alone. I considered changing into Neutrinoman and flying off, but I wasn't properly charged, and I wasn't in the proper mental state.

"What is it?" Licia asked. She had her hand on my arm, but she seemed far away.

"I need to be alone," I said. "Please."

She nodded and walked back to the patio, pulling Valentine back as he was about to follow me. I turned my back and walked down the beach.

———

"A care package, sir," Valentine said, sitting a backpack in front me.

I was several miles down the beach from the adobe casita we had been staying in. It had been several hours since I had left the house.

"Jennifer asks that you remain hydrated," he said. "Licia said that you should eat something."

I smiled. My girls taking care of me. But the smile didn't last long.

"I'll be going now, sir," he said with a brief nod of his head.

I took a deep breath of the salty air and watched as the sun headed towards the horizon. "Is he gone?" I asked.

"Mr. Jordan? Yes. He left shortly after you did."

"And you work for him?" I asked, looking up at the tall man. He had short-cropped grey hair and he wore loose-fitting tan pants and a T-shirt over his fit torso.

"No, sir. I work for you," he said.

"But I don't pay you."

"No, sir."

"Does he?" I asked.

"No, sir."

"Then who pays you?" I asked.

"Not all actions are motivated by monetary remunerations," he said.

I sighed. "Tom sent you."

He nodded.

"Sit down," I said, patting the sand next to me.

He easily folded himself down, his legs crossed, his spine erect.

"And what did Tom give you?" I asked.

He shrugged. It was a minute gesture. "Nothing. He presented a compelling need."

"And that is?" I asked.

"That you needed a bodyguard," he said. "Someone that protects you from physical threats when you are vulnerable."

"Like now?" I asked.

"Yes, sir," he said, the breeze ruffling his short grey hair.

"And if I send you away?" I asked.

"I will monitor threats from a distance," he said, his tone flat.

"Why?" I asked, watching the waves gently caress the shore, breathing the moist air.

"For the same reason they want to give you all that money," he said.

I groaned. "So I can save the world?"

He nodded.

"It's too much, you know," I said, looking into his pale blue eyes. "What you all want from me is too much."

"Yes, sir," he said with a sharp nod. "I agree. But it is no more than you expect from yourself. And it is what is needed."

I remembered the meteor. Flying out to stop it, not believing I could make it back.

"And what if I fail?" I asked.

"You are not the only one in this fight," he said. "Protecting you is *my* best chance of affecting the outcome favorably. Those companies wanting to fund you, that is their best chance. Miss Lopez and Mrs. Johnson, this is their best chance. The other heroes that will gather around you will do so for the same reason. If failure occurs, it is not just you. It is all of us."

"It's too much," I said. "A little over two years ago I was a janitor. Now everyone wants me to save the world. How is that even sane or even possible?"

He smiled and the shadow behind his eyes made me think he had long experience with heavy burdens. "Then lead," he said.

"The leader carries the heaviest burden, but he does not do so alone. Let us stand with you. Let us fight together. And if we fail or succeed, if we live or die, at least we will have stood and fought. At least we will have lived a life we believe in."

He stood up and offered me his hand.

"Let me guess," I said. "That care package was misdirection. If you didn't bring me back, Licia was going to come down here and drag me back."

"Yes, sir," he said with a smile.

I took his hand and he pulled me up and we started walking down the beach.

"So, Heroes Incorporated," I said. "It's kind of a dorky name. I'm not at all fond of the word hero."

"Yes, sir," he said.

"Val, you have to call me Nik."

"Yes, sir," he said.

I laughed, feeling some of the tension ease. I wasn't alone. I had friends. I had Licia. I had a team to assemble, and a planet to save.

EPISODE 6

ELEMENTAL FACTORS

THERE IS MORE ADVENTURE, MORE FUN, MORE NEUTRINOMAN *and Lightningirl* coming soon in episode 6, *Elemental Factors*. Sign up for my newsletter at RobertJMcCarter.com/newsletter and don't miss a thing.

And for the same kind of romantic adventurous fun as *Neutrinoman and Lightningirl* set in post-apocalypse Arizona, check out *Woody and June versus the Apocalypse*. Join the fan club at Woody-AndJune.com and get the first two episodes for free!

———

WOODY AND JUNE VERSUS THE APOCALYPSE

Love and the Apocalypse

When Woody Beckman meets June Medina, neither expects the adventures that will follow. Dedicated go-it-alone survivors, they've learned not to trust anyone in post-zombie-apocalypse Arizona.

But when regular-guy Woody must save tough-as-nails June, they realize that to survive they must learn to trust each other.

As the pair deals with everything from zombies to psychotic, petty, wannabe warlords to the harsh Arizona deserts, they start to realize that they might just prefer facing this crazy world together.

A story of adventure and love and taking things (even the apocalypse) in stride.

Get the first two episodes for free by joining the fan club or go grab Volume 1 with all 7 episodes!

ABOUT THE AUTHOR

Robert J. McCarter is the author of seven novels, three novellas, and dozens of short stories. He is a finalist for the *Writers of the Future* contest and his stories have appeared or are forthcoming in *The Saturday Evening Post, Pulphouse Fiction Magazine, Fiction River, Andromeda Spaceways Inflight Magazine,* and numerous anthologies.

His latest effort is a serialized novel called *Woody and June Versus the Apocalypse,* a story of adventure and love and taking things (even the apocalypse) in stride. Of his novel, *Seeing Forever,* Kirkus Reviews says, "Sci-fi as it should be: engaging, moving, and grand in scope."

He lives in the mountains of Arizona with his amazing wife and his ridiculously adorable dogs.

Find out more at:
robertjmccarter.com

NEUTRINOMAN & LIGHTNINGIRL: A LOVE STORY

- Meteor Attack!
- Toxic Asset
- Protocol X
- Season 1 (Omnibus edition of Episodes 1 - 3)
- Off Book
- Hard Times
- Elemental Factors (coming June, 2020)
- Season 2 (Omnibus edition of Episodes 4-6, coming August , 2020)

Find out the latest at Neutrinoman.com

WOODY AND JUNE VERSUS THE APOCALYPSE

1. Woody and June versus the Wannabe Warlord
2. Woody and June versus the Fungus-Head Zombies
3. Woody and June versus the Grand Canyon
4. Woody and June versus the Ex
5. Woody and June versus the Third Wheel
6. Woody and June versus Phantom Company
7. Woody and June versus the Daring Rescue
8. Volume 1: Episodes 1-7 (all seven episodes for a great price)

Join the Woody and June Fan Club at WoodyAndJune.com